Huckleberry Finn

By

Mark Twain

Retold by Henry Brook
Illustrated by Ian McNee

First published in 2007 by Usborne Publishing Ltd,
Usborne House, 83-85 Saffron Hill,
London EC1N 8RT, England.
www.usborne.com

A catalogue record for this title is available
from the British Library.

Printed in Great Britain

Edited by Jane Chisholm and Rachel Firth
Designed by Sarah Cronin
Series designer: Mary Cartwright
Cover illustration by Ian McNee

CONTENTS

ABOUT
HUCKLEBERRY FINN

Mark Twain published over twenty books in his lifetime, but most readers consider *The Adventures of Huckleberry Finn* to be his masterpiece. It first appeared in 1884 and describes a dangerous journey made by a runaway slave and a young boy through the southern states of America. Jim, the black slave, is trying to reach one of the northern states, where slavery has been abolished and he can live as a free man. But the book's main character, Huck, is on the run from his own family and friends: his vicious, alcoholic father and the 'respectable life' offered by his new guardian, Widow Douglas. It is Huck who narrates the book, and it is through his eyes that we see the violent and vibrant world stretching along the banks of the mighty Mississippi River.

Huckleberry Finn first appeared in one of Twain's earlier novels, *The Adventures of Tom Sawyer* (1876). Set in the sleepy fictional town of St. Petersburg before the turmoil of the American Civil War in 1861, this book follows the adventures of Tom's young gang as they explore the backwoods and hunt for buried treasure. Huck is a tramp, the penniless son of a wandering drunk, who lives off the land and sleeps in a barrel. Other boys envy his 'untamed' existence. Despite his poverty and the regular beatings he receives from his father, Huck is never bitter or self-pitying. He is content with his simple life in the woods. When he and Tom discover a box of gold, Huck even worries that his new riches will bring nothing but problems.

Mark Twain was fascinated by the rough, river tramp he had created in the character of Huck and wanted to give him his own story. He made the daring decision to let Huck narrate the adventure, using all the rich expression and comedy of his own local slang. This bold – and inspired – move gives Twain's novel a unique, American voice and soon earned it a place alongside the country's greatest books. Some critics attacked the author for writing in a coarse and crude style and his book was banned from several libraries. But Huck's account of his adventure rings true, even when he is confronted by corruption, cruelty and the widespread curse of slavery.

Huck was born into a community in the southern states of America that aggressively supported slavery. Slave owners used religion and the law to enforce their message that slavery was necessary and good. Twain's choice of Huck as hero and narrator was difficult for many readers when the book was published, and his portrayal of slavery and racism remains controversial today. As a part of that world, Huck's language and attitudes can seem racist to some modern readers and the novel has been banned in parts of the United

States. But Huck's defenders argue that he challenges and defies the racist attitudes of his times. His struggles with his conscience as he helps Jim to escape are among the most powerful and important scenes in the novel. Forced to choose between freeing his friend or going to hell, Huck finally rejects his racist society and rescues Jim.

Although the book ends with him safe and rich in St. Petersburg, Huck still feels like a restless outsider. He decides to head out to the frontier wilderness of the New Territory for fresh adventures. This open ending shocked many people at the time, but it has inspired many writers. Among them was the famous American novelist Ernest Hemingway, who wrote:

"All modern American literature comes from one book by Mark Twain called Huckleberry Finn..."

A CIVILIZED BOY

You won't know about me unless you've read a book called *The Adventures of Tom Sawyer*. It was Mr. Mark Twain who wrote that book and he told the truth, mostly. He stretched a few things, but I've never met anyone who doesn't tell a few 'stretchers' now and again, except Tom's Aunt Polly or the Widow Douglas, or maybe Mary. You can read about them all in that book of his, which is mostly true as I said before.

The story ends with Tom and me finding the robbers' money hidden in the cave. We got six thousand dollars apiece – in gold. That was quite a sight when it was all piled up. Judge Thatcher banked it for us and the interest worked out at a dollar a day, which is more than a boy knows what to do with. Widow Douglas took me in as her adopted son and set to work 'civilizing' me, but there were too many rules and regulations at her house for my liking. So I returned to my old life – wearing rags and sleeping in a barrel – which suited me just fine. But Tom Sawyer found me and said he was starting a band of robbers and if I lived at the widow's I could join the gang. So I went back.

The widow cried over me and put me in clean new clothes, so all I could do was sweat and itch and hardly breathe. She rang a bell for supper and you had to come right away, but she wouldn't let you eat until she'd grumbled a few words over the dishes. There was nothing wrong with the food that I could see, but I couldn't understand why they didn't just throw everything into the pan and serve it all mixed up. Things taste better to me that way.

After dinner the widow took out her Bible and taught me about the baby Moses floating on his river. I was all in a sweat to find out what happened to him until she told me he'd been dead a long while. After that I stopped listening. I don't see the sense in worrying about dead people.

The widow's sister, Miss Watson, came to live with us and put me to work at her spelling book. She had me at it for an hour until the widow made her stop the torture. I couldn't have taken another minute. The next hour was deadly dull and I started to fidget. Miss Watson would say: "Don't put your feet on the table, Huckleberry," or "Don't yawn and stretch like that, boy. Can't you behave?" Then she told me all about *the bad place* and I said I wished I was there. She got mad at me then, but I didn't mean any harm. All I wanted was a change of scene; I wasn't fussy where it was. She said it was a wicked thing for me to say and she was going to live well and go to *the good place*. That put me right off going there myself, but I kept quiet about that. I didn't want to make trouble.

Miss Watson told me that all you had to do in the good place was to wander around with a harp and sing, forever and forever. I asked her if she thought Tom Sawyer would go there and she shook her head. I was glad about that, because I wanted him and me to stick together.

Miss Watson kept pecking at me about the good place until I was feeling worn down and lonesome. At last it was time for prayers and everyone went to bed. I took a candle up to my room and tried to think of something cheerful, but it was no use. I was so lonely I almost wished I were dead. The stars were shining and the woods were full of strange noises. I heard the wind whispering among the trees, like a ghost who can't find any rest and has to go around bothering folks. I got so sad and scared I wished I had someone with me. Then I saw a spider on my arm and I brushed him off without thinking, right into the candle flame. I didn't need anyone to tell me that killing a poor spider brings the worst kind of luck and I got so jumpy I was almost shaking my clothes off. After a long time I heard the clock in the town booming twelve times and after that the night was still. A twig broke, down in the dark between the trees and something called: "Mia-yow, mia-yow." My heart jumped for joy when I heard that sound. I put out the light, scrambled out of the window and dropped onto the shed. When I reached the ground, Tom Sawyer was standing there waiting.

We tiptoed through the trees, stooping down so the branches wouldn't brush our heads. But, as we crept past the kitchen door, I tripped over a root and made a noise. One of Miss Watson's slaves, Jim, was sitting in the doorway, framed by the light. He looked up and stared out into the darkness, listening for almost a minute.

"Well, who's there?" he asked finally.

He listened some more and then he came tiptoeing out and stood right between us. It was too dark to see anything but he was so close he could have touched me. Crouching there, I got an itch on my ankle but I couldn't tend to it – I knew he'd hear me if I scratched it. My ear began to itch and then I got another itch between my shoulder blades. I thought I'd die if I couldn't start scratching. I've noticed the same thing plenty of times since. If you're at a funeral or in fine company, or trying to sleep when you're not sleepy, you start to itch in a thousand places.

"Speak up now," said Jim suddenly. "I know I heard something. Well, I'm going to sit right here until I hear it again."

He sat down between us and leaned against a tree. My nose began to itch, on the outside, inside and underneath, and soon my eyes were streaming with tears. But I didn't dare scratch. I was in this misery for six or seven minutes – though it seemed a lot longer – until I thought I couldn't stand another second. Just then, Jim began breathing heavily and started to snore – and I was saved.

Tom smacked his lips to give me the sign we could creep away, but when we'd crawled ten feet off he stopped. In a whisper he told me it would be a fine joke to tie Jim to the tree. Well, I didn't want Jim to start shouting and wake the house, so I said no. Then Tom said he needed some candles from the kitchen. I didn't want to risk it but Tom wouldn't listen, so we slipped in and took three candles. Tom left five cents on the table as payment and we hurried outside. I was in a sweat to get away but nothing would stop Tom from playing some prank on Jim. He crawled off into the dark and was gone for what seemed like ages. When he got back we cut along the path and ended up on the top of the hill on the other side of the house.

Tom told me he'd slipped Jim's hat off his head and left it hanging on a branch. Afterwards, Jim told everyone some witches must have put him in a trance, rode him all over the state and left the hat there to show who'd done it. Jim was a great believer in witches and their magic powers. The next time he told the story, those witches took him all the way to New Orleans, and he went further each time he told it.

Pretty soon, Jim was going all around the world and his back was covered in saddle sores. He was proud of his adventure. Other slaves came from miles around to hear the tale, standing there with their mouths open while Jim gave them all the details. And if Jim came in and found some other slave telling stories about magic and witches around the fire, he'd huff and puff and say: "And just what do *you* know about witches?"

He even wore our five-cent coin around his neck on a string and said it was a charm given to him personally by the devil. All Jim had to do was say a few words and the devil would come – but Jim never told anyone what those words might be. Slaves came over to stare at that coin, but they didn't dare touch it since it had been stroked by Lucifer. Jim was ruined as a servant, because he got so full of himself with all his devilish adventures and wild rides with witches.

Standing on the hill we looked down on our small town of St. Petersburg and the mile-wide Mississippi River, still and grand in the moonlight. We went down the hill to where Jo Harper and two or three other boys were waiting for us, ready with a flat-bottomed boat. Two miles downriver we landed and Tom led us to a secret hole hidden by some bushes. We lit candles and crawled inside, following Tom through great caves and twisting passages until at last he stopped.

"Anyone who wants to join my gang of robbers," he whispered to us, "has to make an oath and sign for it in blood."

Everyone was willing, so Tom took a piece of paper from his pocket and read the oath he'd drawn up. It was full of wild language and murderous threats to kill any boy who revealed the gang's secrets. We all thought it was about the best oath we'd ever come across. Tom owned up that he'd borrowed parts of it from all the pirate and robber books he liked to read.

One boy said we should kill the families of any boy who betrayed the gang, and there I hit a snag. Ben Rogers said I didn't have any family to kill.

"What about his pap?" cried Tom.

"But where's he gone to?" asked Ben. "He used to sleep with the hogs in the tannery yard but nobody's seen him for more than a year."

They talked it over and it looked like I was out of the club. I was ready to cry when suddenly an idea came to me.

"There's Miss Watson," I offered. "You could kill her if I squeal."

"She'll do," they all cried at once, and then every boy pricked his finger with a pin to sign the membership form. It took hours to decide on what crimes the gang should commit, and whether we should murder people or just hold them for ransom. By the time I was climbing through my bedroom window it was almost daylight. My new clothes were all greasy and covered in clay and I was as tired as a dog.

THE HOMECOMING

Miss Watson gave me a good scolding the next morning, on account of my dirty clothes. The widow didn't say a word. She cleaned off the grease and dirt and looked so sad I decided to behave for a while – if I could. Then Miss Watson asked me to pray with her and I tried. She told me if I prayed every day, I'd get what I asked for, but it didn't work. I prayed for some fish-hooks but they never came, and when I asked Miss Watson to try for me she said I was a fool.

I walked deep into the woods and had a long think about this praying business. If people can get what they want by praying, why are so many people poor and unhappy? I asked the widow about it and she told me that praying brings a person 'spiritual gifts' and not fish-hooks. She said I had to be good and kind to everyone I met and never think of myself, but I couldn't see the advantage in that. Perhaps I was just too ignorant and low-down for the good place, but I decided I'd go if I got the invitation.

We played at robbers for a month or two and then the gang broke up. Tom Sawyer was always planning new schemes and promising us riches, but he never delivered the goods. One time we raided a picnic gathering in the woods and Tom said it was a camel train loaded with diamonds and gold bars. It looked like a plain Sunday school outing to me, but Tom said I'd been enchanted by an evil magician and I couldn't trust my own eyes. He said I should read a book called *Don Quixote* and then I'd understand all about enchanters and their spells. We had a long talk about magic and genies after that and I even took an old lamp out to the woods to see if I could make a genie come out of it. I rubbed at that lamp until my arm almost fell off, but nothing happened.

Four months went by and winter set in. I'd been going to school most days and I could read and write a little. At first I hated the lessons, but they got easier. Life at the widow's got easier too, and although I still liked the old ways best I was beginning to like the new ones too.

But one morning I overturned the saltcellar on the breakfast table and I knew it was a sure sign I was due some bad luck. When I was climbing over the stile at the end of the garden I noticed some footprints in the snow. It looked as though someone had been pacing around there, watching and waiting. I was curious so I crouched down to study the tracks. When I saw a cross in one of the footprints, I stood up and started running. I knew that cross all too well. It was made of nails hammered into a boot heel, and it was a charm to keep off the devil.

I ran all the way to Judge Thatcher's house.

"Why, my boy," he declared, "you're out of breath.

What's your hurry?"

"I've got news for you, sir," I replied.

"I've got news too," he smiled. "Your six-month interest payment has come in. Shall I bank it with the rest?"

"Keep it, sir," I said. "I want you to have every cent of it, and the six thousand too."

"Do you really mean that, Huck?" he cried in amazement. "But why?"

"I can't tell you, sir," I answered. "Just take it all."

"Perhaps you want to sign it over to me?" he suggested. "Well, that should be possible."

The judge wrote a few words on a piece of paper and handed me a silver dollar. "Sign this contract," he said, "and take this dollar as a token payment, to make it official."

So I signed and left. I knew trouble was coming my way and all the money in the world wasn't going to help me. When I went up to my room that night, Pap was sitting in the chair waiting for me.

I was always scared of him before, when he used to beat me. But after I got over the shock of seeing him there, I realized I wasn't scared of him at all. He was about fifty years old and he looked every bit of it. His hair was long, matted and greasy. It was black as coal, the same as his beard, and his bright eyes glared at me through the tangle. What I could see of his face made my flesh crawl. The skin was a sickly white, like the belly of a toad or a dead fish. As for his clothes – just rags, that was all. His boots were so broken and torn I could see two toes sticking out, and his old black hat was caved in and ruined.

I put the candle down and saw that the window was open. He must have climbed up over the shed.

"Think you're a big shot now, don't you," he spat at me, when all the staring was over.

"Maybe," I said, "maybe not."

"Don't give me any lip, boy," he snapped. "You've lost your manners while I've been away. I suppose that's what happens when you hang around a school, like you've been doing. Who told you to start fooling around trying to get educated?"

"The widow told me," I replied.

"She's got no business meddling," he grumbled. "You stay away from that school, do you hear? We never had any readers in this family and I won't put up with it from you. If I catch you around that school I'll tan you black and blue."

He sat there mumbling and growling for a moment before he started up again. "And what are you doing sleeping in a bed," he snapped, "and your own father's got to sleep with the hogs in the tannery? Well, I'll take you down a peg or two, yes I will. They say you're rich. How'd that happen?"

"It didn't," I told him. "They lied."

"Don't get sassy with me. I've been in town two days and all I hear about is how rich you are. I even heard it upriver, that's why I came back. You'll get me that money tomorrow."

"I can't," I answered. "I haven't got any money."

"I know," he sneered, "Judge Thatcher's looking after it for you. Well, I'll ask him for it and I'll make him pay. How much have you got in your pocket?"

"One dollar," I told him. "And I want it."

"It doesn't make any difference what you want," he barked, "pass it over."

He took it and bit it to see if it was the real thing. "I haven't had a drink all day," he grumbled. "I'm going into town for some whiskey."

Pap climbed awkwardly through the open window and rested his weight on the roof of the shed. "You stay away from that school," he warned me in a snarl, before he dropped to the ground. "I don't want you getting any more of these airs and graces. You understand?"

In the morning he was drunk and he went to see Judge Thatcher, but he couldn't make him hand over the money. Widow Douglas tried to get custody of me, but we had a new county judge and he was dead set against breaking up a family. He didn't know Pap.

The new judge invited my old man into his house and Pap said he was going to give up drinking and lead a decent, sober life from that day on. Pap broke down in tears and said he'd fooled away too many precious years already, and soon everyone in the house was weeping and the judge hugged the old man and gave him some new clothes. Pap said he was 'reformed' and all he needed was a second chance – and a little sympathy. So the judge made him a guest in his house and Pap cried some more and thanked him and hugged him again before going up to bed.

But in the night Pap got thirsty and he shinned down the side of the house and went into town. He traded his new clothes for some rotgut whiskey and, when he was good and drunk, he smashed all the furniture in his bedroom and fell out of the window. Pap broke his left arm in two places. The new judge was disappointed, to say the least. He said the only way to reform a man like Pap was with a shotgun.

When he got better, Pap found a lawyer and went after Judge Thatcher again for the money. He went after me too, thrashing me if he caught me going to school. Then he started hanging around the widow's house, watching for me, until the widow told him she'd make trouble for him if he didn't leave us in peace. That made him mad. "I'm the boss of Huck Finn," Pap shouted. "You wait and see." He caught me one morning in the spring and took me upriver in a skiff. We crossed over to the Illinois shore, to where the woods are lonely, thick and dark. Pap had a log cabin there, so well hidden in the timber you'd never find it unless you knew where to look.

CABIN FEVER

Pap kept me with him all the time and when he locked the cabin door at night he went to sleep with the key under his head. He had a gun – stolen, I figured – and we fished and hunted and lived off the land. Every week or so he went down to the store at the ferry, three miles away, and traded our fish and game for a jug of whiskey. When he got drunk, I always took a beating. The widow found out where I was and sent a man to get me, but Pap drove him off with the gun. After that I got used to my life in the cabin. I even started to like it, lazing around and not going to school. My new clothes were soon in rags and I remembered how comfortable the old ways were. I had no wish to return to the widow's, where everything was starched and scrubbed and I had to say my prayers every night.

It was a good life in the woods – except for Pap's beatings. He used to thrash me with a stick and I was always covered in bruises. Then he started going away 'on business' and locking me in the cabin. Once I didn't see him for three whole days and I thought he'd been drowned in an accident and I'd die of thirst – or loneliness. I decided to escape as soon as I could.

I'd had plenty of time to explore that cabin, looking for a way out, but it was built like a prison. The windows were so tight a dog couldn't slip through, and the door was made of thick, oak slabs. I didn't have a knife or any other tools, but after hours of searching I found a rusty old saw, hidden in the rafters. There was an old blanket hanging over one wall of the cabin and I crawled under it and started sawing away at the lowest log. If I could remove it, there would be just enough of a gap for me to wriggle free. I was almost through when I heard Pap's gun away in the woods, so I hid everything behind the blanket and jumped up.

He was in a foul temper when he burst in – as usual – and he started grumbling about his lawyer and Judge Thatcher and Widow Douglas. Things weren't going his way and it looked as though the widow might win custody of me and take me back to her house. This news made me shudder – I didn't want to be 'civilized' again if I could help it.

Pap started swearing and shouting. He said he knew a hiding place, deep in the woods, where the widow would never find me. Then he made me go out to the skiff and bring in some supplies he'd bought: bacon, corn and whiskey. While I was tramping along the path I made up my mind to get away that night – from Pap *and* the widow. I thought I'd be better off alone, hunting and fishing and sleeping rough. Pap was bound to get drunk that evening. When he passed out, I could make a run for it.

We had dinner and then Pap went to work on the whiskey jug. He got all fired up and started roaring about the government and the state of the nation and all the injustices he'd suffered. I was just waiting for him to fall asleep so I could slip away, but when he did finally tumble into his blankets he thrashed around and moaned like a tormented man. I got so tired waiting for him to settle, I dropped off myself without even blowing out the candle.

I don't know how long I was asleep but I woke to hear Pap screaming. He was brushing his legs and dancing around, talking about snakes crawling all over him. But if there were any snakes in that room they were invisible. Then he crashed to the floor and started trembling and grabbing at the air, saying the devils were holding him down. Suddenly he was quiet and I could hear the owls and the wolves off in the woods and I was scared. Pap jumped up and his eyes were flashing. "It's you," he screeched. "You're the Angel of Death."

"No, Pap," I cried. "I'm Huck."

He whipped out a knife and started chasing me around the cabin. "Come here, you evil ghost," he called. "I'll kill you and then you won't bother me again, you devil."

There was nothing for it but to run. We darted around and around the cabin and one time he almost got me. But I was quicker than him and soon he dropped down exhausted, leaning heavily against the door.

"I'll take a rest, then I'll finish you off," he mumbled, and fell into a dead sleep.

I found the gun and took up a post on the far side of the cabin, with the barrel aimed directly at his chest. Then I waited, with my heart pounding and my finger on the trigger.

"Hey, boy, what are you doing with that gun?"

I opened my eyes, blinking in the morning sunlight. Pap was standing over me looking sour – and sick. I guessed he'd forgotten all about his madness in the night, so I said: "Somebody tried to get in."

"Why didn't you wake me up?" he asked.

"I tried but you wouldn't budge."

"Well, all right," he coughed. "Now go and check the lines and see if there's any fish hooked we can have for breakfast."

I ran outside and followed the path to the river. The water was running high and there was a lot of driftwood and other debris snagged along the bank. It was a *rise* – when the river swells with a sudden flood.

I remembered some of the rich pickings I'd had from a rise the year before. Floodwater carries things downstream, making them free salvage for anyone who finds them. Suddenly I spotted a canoe bobbing past – a real beauty about twelve feet long. I dived into the river as quick as a frog and swam out to it, half expecting some practical joker to be lying down in the bottom, ready to sit up and laugh at me. But she was empty, so I climbed in and paddled her to shore.

I was going to give her to Pap but, when I ran into a little creek all covered in hanging vines, I had another idea. Why not hide her away, ready for my escape? I could float down the river fifty miles and the old man would never find me.

We had five catfish off the lines for breakfast and when we'd eaten our fill we both stretched out to rest.

"You wake me up the next time a man comes," Pap said, lifting his head up from his blankets. "Wake me up and I'll shoot him. If he's prowling around he could be a killer."

Pap went off to sleep, but my mind was racing with a new plan. I didn't want the widow or Pap on my trail for the rest of my life. Pap's warning had given me an idea and I thought I could fix it so nobody would ever think of searching for me.

We were up at noon, looking for salvage in the rise. When Pap saw part of a raft going by, we rowed out to it and hauled it in. There were nine logs roped together and Pap wanted to ferry them to the lumberyard and sell them without delay. He locked me in the cabin and took off with the skiff in the afternoon. Before he was halfway across the river, I'd finished sawing through the log in the cabin wall and was putting my plan into action.

I gathered all our supplies – including Pap's gun – and loaded them into my canoe. Then I fixed the sawed log back into the wall so you could hardly see it had been tampered with. Next, I scattered sawdust over the ground to cover my footprints, and then I went out hunting for a bird to shoot. But I was lucky – I came across a wild pig. I killed him and dragged him back to the cabin where I hacked down the door with the woodpile axe.

Dragging the pig inside, I spread his blood all over the floor. When the place was dripping with gore, I got a sack and some rocks. I dragged the dead animal across the grass to the river – weighted down in the sack – and rolled him in. The marks and bloodstains on the grass were clear to see. It was only a pity that Tom Sawyer wasn't there to help me add some flourishes. There's nobody like Tom Sawyer for adding the flourishes to a scheme.

When I'd finished, I lay in the bottom of my canoe and watched the moon come up. Pap and the sheriff would think robbers had killed me. They'd drag the river for my body and hunt the woods for the murderers – while I floated off on the tide. I nudged the canoe away from the bank. The sight of the mighty river rushing by took my breath away.

The flood carried me off, spinning and turning me under the great night sky. In no time at all I saw

a black shape rising up out of the water ahead, like a steamboat with no lights. It was Jackson's Island, a deserted hump of rock and trees only a few miles down from St. Petersburg. If I stopped on the island, I could sneak across to my old town for anything I needed without being discovered, So, I ran the canoe into a muddy bank and hid her in a wall of willow branches. Then I climbed into the woods and sat on a log, gazing at the lights twinkling away in the distance. Dawn was coming up when I finally laid my head down to rest.

RUNAWAYS

I woke with the sun already high in the sky, feeling refreshed and well satisfied with life. My bed was the lush grass in a sun-dappled grove of trees, with a breeze whispering in the leaves above. It was all so lazy and comfortable I couldn't stir myself to fix breakfast and I was just dozing off again when I heard a rumbling *boom* upriver. When I heard it again I got to my feet and looked through some bushes. I could see the landing where the ferry ties up near the town, and there were clouds of white smoke rolling across the water. The townspeople were firing a cannon from the ferryboat, thinking the vibrations from the blast would bring my dead body floating to the surface.

I watched the boat working its way downriver, and then I realized I could have a look at the people on board as they drifted by. There were some thick bushes down by the shore and I hid behind them, peering through a little gap in the branches.

The boat came so close to shore they could have put a plank out and walked across to meet me. Everybody was there on the deck – Pap, Judge Thatcher and Tom Sawyer among them – and I could hear two ladies discussing my murder in excited voices.

Then the captain fired his cannon and the blast almost deafened me. When I came to my senses the boat had gone and I was alone again. So my plan had worked and I was safe. After shooting up the river they'd call off the search, I figured. I made myself busy unloading the canoe and putting up a respectable tent made of thick blankets.

For three days I roamed around the island, fishing, collecting wild berries and exploring. It was a quiet and lonely life but I was happy on the whole. On the fourth day I was out hunting with the gun when I almost stepped on a great, fat snake. He slid into the bushes and I chased after him, thinking it would be safer to kill him than share the woods with him. I ran straight into a clearing and the remains of a campfire. The ashes were still smoking.

My heart was up in my mouth as I tiptoed out of there. I kept watching and listening all the way back to my own camp and then I quickly loaded all my valuables into the canoe and climbed up a tree. It seemed as good a place as any to hide.

I stayed up there for three hours, until it got dark. That night I tried to sleep in the canoe, out of sight behind the willows, but I was so scared and uncomfortable the sleep didn't do me any good. A few hours before dawn I decided I couldn't go on living like a coward. I figured it would be better to brave it out and search for any intruders. If I spotted anyone, I could either turn myself in or make a run for it. I felt better right away.

I untied the canoe and quietly paddled down the length of the island. When I got level to where I'd seen the fire, I tied up and started making my way through the woods, holding the gun barrel out before me. At first I couldn't find my way to the clearing, but then I saw the glimmer of firelight up ahead. Moving slowly, I poked my nose through the bushes and saw a man lying on the ground by the embers. He had a blanket wrapped around his head to act as a pillow; he was so close to the fire he was almost on it.

I was only six feet away from the stranger and my hands were shaking as though they were ice-cold. At last, daylight started to show through the trees above and I saw the man suddenly stretch and pull the blanket away from his face. It was Miss Watson's slave, Jim.

Well, I was so overjoyed to see him I skipped into the clearing and shouted his name. But, instead of greeting me with a smile, Jim screamed and begged for mercy. "Don't hurt me, you mean old ghost," he cried. "I always liked dead people and tried to help them when I could. Now get back into that river where you belong."

It didn't take long for me to explain I wasn't dead and that I was glad to have a companion in the world of the living. A boy can only stand so much loneliness.

"How long have you been on the island?" I asked him.

"Since the night after you were murdered. What about you?" "I came the same night I was killed. Now build up that fire and we'll have some breakfast."

"What's the use in a cooking fire when there's nothing but berries to cook?" Jim said with a frown.

"Is that all you've had to eat in three days?" I said.

"It is and I could eat a horse."

"Well, I've got plenty of food up at my camp. And I'll bet there's some catfish on my hooks we can add to the pan."

After breakfast we lay back in the grass and stared up at the clouds. I told Jim everything about my escape and he said it was a fine plan – worthy of Tom Sawyer even. But when I asked him what he was doing on the island he looked uneasy.

"You wouldn't tell on me, Huck?" he asked.

"Of course not," I replied.

"Well, I ran off."

"Jim!"

"You promised not to tell," he reminded me.

"I know I did and I won't. Even though people might despise me for keeping quiet. Why'd you do it?"

"Miss Watson treated me pretty rough," said Jim, "but she always said she wouldn't sell me to the New Orleans traders. They're the worst people a slave can go to, Huck, working a man to death. But lately I've noticed a trader hanging around the town and one night I overheard Miss Watson tell the widow she could get eight hundred dollars for me. It was too much money to refuse. The widow tried to ask her not to do it, but I didn't wait to see how it turned out.

"I slipped away and hid in some trees by the river, hoping to steal a boat. But I was there all night and had no luck. When the sun came up, I heard people moving around on the shore, talking about how you'd been murdered. I was sorry to hear it, Huck, and it's good to see you alive and well.

"I waited all day and when it got dark I started walking. But I knew the tracker dogs would find me if I didn't get in the water, so I pushed out into the stream, paddling behind a log. I saw a big raft coming downstream and I thought I'd steal a ride on her so I swam up close. The rafters were all in the middle of the raft and it was pitch dark. I climbed onboard and nobody saw me.

"But my luck turned when a rafter came over with a lantern. I dived back in the river and sighted the island not far off, so I swam to it. And I've been hiding in these woods ever since."

We went exploring that afternoon and discovered a cave hidden away in the middle of the island. Jim saw some birds flying a few yards through the trees, settling on a branch and then flying off again. He said it was a sign that rain was coming. Jim knew all the magic signs. We carried our camp supplies up to the cave so we'd have shelter if there was a storm.

Later that day the sky turned black and it rained with a fury. I've never seen the wind blow so wild. Lightning bolts lit up the woods and the thunder made the ground shake. The noise tumbled across the sky like the sound of an empty barrel rolling down a flight of stairs. But we were warm and dry in our cave.

The river kept on rising for ten or twelve days and the water came lapping over the banks. We paddled around the low parts of the island in our canoe and on every branch you could see rabbits, snakes, turtles and other animals driven off the ground by the flood.

One night we found a raft made of pine planks, about a dozen feet wide and sixteen feet long. We tied it up and hid it in the willows. Another night we saw a timber house floating by. We paddled out to her in the canoe but it was too dark to see inside, so we waited for the dawn to come. At first light we peered in at the window and I could see a table and a bed and something lying on the floor. It looked like a man.

"Hello, you," Jim shouted, but there was no answer.

"I reckon he's dead," Jim whispered. "I'll go and see."

He climbed in and walked carefully across to the body. "He's dead all right," Jim called. "Shot in the back. Come and see, Huck, but don't look in his face. It's too awful for your young eyes."

"Cover him up," I answered. "I don't want to see it."

The floor was littered with playing cards, whiskey bottles and some masks made of black cloth. We scouted around and carried our booty back to the canoe: a tin lantern, a worn old quilt, candles, tin cups, buttons, fish lines, a coat, men's shirts and a girl's dress, a horseshoe, a fiddle bow and a wooden leg. The straps on the leg were broken and it was too long for me and too short for Jim, but it was a good enough leg so we took it anyway.

We got the whole load to the island and hauled it up to the cave. Picking through it, we found eight dollars stitched into the lining of the coat, a real stroke of luck that only added to the mystery of the house. I wanted to talk about the dead man and his killer, but Jim wouldn't discuss it. He told me it was bad luck to talk about a man who wasn't buried properly. Jim said that that man was more likely to go out haunting than a corpse who was warm and snug in his coffin. I didn't ask about it again.

DRESSING UP

After two weeks on the island, I was feeling restless and ready for a new adventure. I told Jim I'd slip up to town when it got dark and find out the news. He thought that was a fine idea. "Why don't you go in disguise?" he suggested. "It might be safer. You could wear that dress we found in the house and pass as a girl."

The dress was a fair fit and we fixed a sunbonnet over my forehead so it was hard to see my face. I spent the afternoon getting used to the outfit and after sunset I set out in the canoe.

The river current carried me in to the bottom of town and I tied up and started along the bank. There was an old hut on the edge of town that had a light burning in the window. I knew nobody had lived there for years, so I peeked in the window out of curiosity. A woman I didn't recognize was sitting by the table knitting. This was a piece of luck. I'd been worried that my voice would give me away to anyone in the town who knew me. But I was certain I could fool this stranger into thinking I was a girl – even if I did have an uncommonly deep voice. I knocked on the door.

"Come in," called the woman, and I did. "Take a chair," she said. "And who might you be?"

"Sarah Williams," I answered.

"You a local girl?" she asked.

"Never been here before," I replied. "I've come to tell my uncle that my mother's sick. He lives in the upper part of this town, I believe."

"But it's late in the evening," the woman said, "and you've still got a way to go. You can spend the night here, child. Why don't you take off your bonnet?"

"All I need is a little rest, thank you. I'm not scared of the dark."

She told me her husband would be back in an hour and that on his return she would ask him to escort me to my uncle's house. Then she started jawing about her family and how she'd only been here two weeks and she wasn't sure if she liked it. I heard so many details concerning her life and family I was beginning to despair, but then she finally got on to Pap and my murder.

"Who did it, do they know?" I asked her in an excited whisper.

"They almost lynched his father for the crime," she cried. "But he was saved when the finger of guilt pointed to a runaway slave by the name of Jim. This slave took off the same night as the murder and there's three hundred dollars of reward money for anyone who brings him back to face justice. Old Finn borrowed some cash from Judge Thatcher and disappeared with two hard-looking strangers, saying he'd bring the slave back or die trying. But he hasn't been seen since and people are saying he most likely killed the boy and staged the whole robbery so he could get his sly hands on Huck's money. There's no proof of that, mind you."

"What about the runaway slave?" I said. "Do people think he's innocent now?"

"Not everybody."

"He must be long gone," I sighed.

"You think so?" she asked craftily. "You know Jackson's Island? No, of course you don't, being a stranger, but you must have passed it on your way up here. Well, I'm sure I saw some smoke drifting up from that island last week. People say it's uninhabited, but where did that smoke come from? I've got a feeling that runaway slave might be hiding over there and I've told my husband to take a look the first chance he gets."

I couldn't listen to all this talk without my hands shaking. To keep them busy I picked a needle off the table and started trying to thread it. The woman looked at me strangely.

"Is your husband going out there soon?" I asked, trying not to gulp my words.

"He's gone to get a boat and a gun and he's rowing out there after midnight. What did you say your name was again, honey?"

"Mary Williams," I mumbled.

"But you said it was Sarah," she cried.

"Sarah's my first name," I replied, trying not to panic. "But some people call me by my middle name, Mary."

"Come now," she asked softly, "what's your real name? Is it Bob, or Tom, or something more along those lines?"

I was shaking like a leaf as I replied: "Please, ma'am, don't poke fun at a poor little girl like me."

"It's all right, child," she told me. "I've guessed your secret. You're an apprentice boy from one of the farms downriver, on the run from a cruel master, I'll bet. What's your real name?"

"George Peters," I told her, trying to think fast. "And everything you said is true. I've been treated badly since my parents died last year. The local court made me work for a mean old farmer who lives out in the wilderness. He beat me if I did a thing wrong and I ran away three days ago."

"I knew it," she cried, smiling at how clever she had been. "And you stole that dress to throw the farmer's men off the scent if they stopped you on the road?"

"That's right, every word of it. My uncle will take me in when I explain things, I'm sure of it. But I should hurry to see him before he locks his house up for the night."

"Don't worry, I'll keep your secret safe, George," she said kindly. "Let me fix you a snack for your journey. Now take my advice and don't go pretending to be a girl around a woman again. When I saw you trying to thread that needle, I guessed you were a boy in a second."

She gave me a hunk of bread and cheese, wished me good luck and waved me off into the night. I hurried fifty yards up the track before darting back to the canoe and paddling for the island. When I was halfway across, I heard the town clock tolling across the water – eleven times. I landed and ran all the way to the cave. Jim was sound asleep on the ground.

"Jump to it, Jim," I shouted. "They're after us."

Thirty minutes later, we were shoving the raft out from her willow hideaway, loaded with all our supplies and the canoe. We didn't look back and we didn't say a word.

ON THE WATER

When the first streak of day began to show in the sky, we stopped at a sandbar island close to the Illinois shore of the river. These sandbars are low banks of river sediment and mud, sometimes covered with cottonwood trees and scrub. We chopped enough branches to cover the raft so it couldn't be seen from the main channel, then we waited through the heat of the day, watching all the rafts and steamboats plying their way up and down the river.

As soon as it got dark, Jim set to work stripping the raft and building a sturdy 'wigwam' out of the planks, to give us shelter from sun and rain – and hide us from prying eyes. Then he made a floor for the wigwam, a foot higher than the raft, so it would be out of reach of any waves made by passing steamboats. He spread dirt on the floor and said we could have a fire there if the weather turned cold. Then he put up a post and attached our lantern to it. We didn't want to get run over by steamboats because they hadn't seen us.

When everything was ready with our new home we left the sandbar and started downriver. We fished and talked things over, taking a swim now and again to keep ourselves awake. It was kind of solemn, drifting down the big, still river, looking up at the stars.

We soon got used to a routine of resting in the wigwam during the day and working the raft at night. In the evening I'd come ashore at a village and buy some corn or bacon for our dinner. Sometimes I lifted a chicken, if I came across one away from his roost. I took watermelons, pumpkins and fresh corn too and we landed in the mornings to pick fruit for our breakfast. Pap always said there wasn't any harm in 'borrowing' things to eat, but the widow said it was no better than stealing. Jim thought there was some truth in both these claims, so we decided to meet them halfway. We crossed a few items off our borrowing list – but I confess they were just the things we didn't like to eat in the first place.

On the fifth night we passed the city of St. Louis. It was like the whole world lit up. In St. Petersburg they used to say there were thirty thousand people in St. Louis, but I never believed it until I saw that wonderful spread of lights along the banks.

Five nights after that we hit a storm and we had to hide from the lightning and rain in the wigwam. When the lightning flashed you could see the river stretching away for miles ahead. With the storm raging around us, I caught sight of a steamboat caught on a rock, still and ghostly in the middle of the stream. We were heading straight for her.

"It's a wreck, Jim," I cried. "Let's land on her." I couldn't think of a better adventure than exploring a shipwreck during a terrible storm, but Jim was dead set against it.

"It's none of our business disturbing this wreck," he complained. "Besides, there might be a watchman on board."

"It's too dangerous a job for any watchman," I replied. "In this storm she could slip off that rock and sink any second. I'm sure she's been abandoned, and just think of the treasure we might find in the captain's stateroom. Stick a candle in your pocket and be brave, Jim, because I can't rest until we give her a rummaging. I only wish Tom Sawyer was here to join us in the adventure."

Jim grumbled but he soon gave in. A moment later we'd tied the raft to one of the steamboat paddles and we were creeping along the decks to the front cabins. We went through a doorway and stepped into a long corridor. At the far end I could see a light gleaming in one of the rooms.

"Don't do, it, boys," a voice screamed. "I swear I won't tell."

Then another man shouted: "I'm not taking any more chances with you, Jim Turner. Every time we do a job you always try to get the bigger share, threatening to squeal if we don't pay up. That won't happen again."

The next second, Jim was tiptoeing off to the raft. But I couldn't leave before I knew what kind of adventure was taking place here on the wreck. As I crawled to the light, I saw a man lying on the bare board floor, tied at the hands and wrists. Two other men were standing over him – one held a lantern and the other was pointing a pistol.

"Let's finish him," growled the man with the gun.

"I'd like to, Bill," said the man with the lamp. "He's a lying skunk and he wouldn't think twice about killing us if he needed to. But I reckon we've scared him so badly he won't threaten us again. Put your gun away."

"I still say we should kill him, Jake," Bill shouted.

"No," snapped Jake. "I want him alive."

The man on the floor started blubbering: "Oh, bless your heart for your mercy."

"Let's have a word in private," said Jake and he hung up his lamp and motioned to Bill to follow him. I watched in horror as they stepped right in my direction and I had to hurry back into one of the cabins. They stepped in too and shut the door behind them. It was so dark they couldn't see me, curled up in one of the bunks on the wall, but I knew exactly where they were. They were so close I could smell the whiskey on their breath.

"After tonight," Bill started in a whisper, "we can never trust that man again. I say we put him out of his misery."

"And so do I," replied Jake.

"Well, let's do it then," Bill muttered in surprise.

"No," said Jake. "Let's get the wreck to do it for us. I don't want the blood of a man on my hands if I can help it. We'll hunt around for any more booty, then leave him here tied up. When the storm finally breaks the ship free from the rock, he'll sink without a trace."

"What if it stays stuck?" asked Bill.

"We can watch from the safety of the bank," replied Jake. "If the storm passes and the wreck's still here, we'll come back and do the murder."

Bill agreed to this plan and the two men started searching the other cabins for plunder. I darted back through the gloom and lightning and found Jim waiting for me at the stern of the boat.

"Quick, Jim," I whispered, "there's a man's life at stake. We have to find the robbers' boat and set it adrift. If we trap them here they won't dare to do the killing. When the storm dies down the sheriff will be out to check the wreck and he'll find them. Their boat must be tied up somewhere. I'll start looking along the port side; you can move up the starboard side from our raft."

"The raft?" Jim howled as he looked over the side. "What raft? She's broken lose and we're stuck on this wreck with a gang of murderers."

I almost fainted when I heard this news. All our supplies and materials had gone down the river. But there was no time to get weepy-eyed about it. We had to find that other boat without delay – for our own escape.

It took ten minutes of scrambling around in the dark before we saw it – a skiff, bobbing alongside the cabin section of the wreck. I was about to jump down into her when a door opened only a foot from my head. A man stuck his head out and then quickly pulled it back inside. "Put that light out first," he called to his friend.

Jake and Bill stepped down into the boat, while I hung grimly onto the side of the wreck.

"Shove off," growled Jake.

"Wait," said Bill. "Did you go through his pockets?"

"No," replied Jake. "I thought *you* did."

"Back we go," said Bill. "He's got his share of the job hidden somewhere. There's no sense leaving it."

The door slammed behind them and I was down in their boat in less than a second. Jim tumbled in after me and I hacked through the mooring rope with a clasp knife I had in my pocket.

We went gliding along in silence, too scared to say a word or even draw a full breath. A few seconds later we were below the wreck and she was soaking into the darkness behind us. But when I turned to look, I saw a light sparkling in the gloom – the lantern searching for the lost boat. For the first time that night, I worried about leaving those men on the boat, even if they were murderers. So, I said to Jim: "Let's stop when we see a light on the shore. I'll make up a story and get someone to go out and get those men. They can hang when their time comes, all right and proper."

But the storm was raging again and it was a long time before we saw any sign of life along the river. We kept a sharp lookout for our own raft and soon enough we spotted her, lit up by a lightning flash. The robbers had left their plunder in the belly of the skiff and we quickly loaded it onto the raft. After ten minutes or more, I noticed a light on the banks and I told Jim to meet me a mile downriver while I rowed the skiff to the shore.

I came up to a ferryboat and paddled around looking for the night watchman. He was snoring away in a hammock but he woke up when I gave his shoulder two or three little shoves.

"My family's stranded on the wreck, sir," I wailed, my eyes suddenly streaming with tears.

"What wreck?" he cried, rolling out of the hammock in a flash.

"The one upriver," I replied, "the steamboat."

"I know the one," said the man. "And what were they doing going aboard?"

"We lost the steering oar on our raft, sir," I told him, "and smashed into the hull of the wreck. We've been yelling for help, but the river flows so wide there, nobody on the banks could hear us. Well, I told my pap I thought I was a strong enough swimmer to reach the shore. I made it and found this boat and now I'm here."

"There's a tavern along the road," he shouted, pulling on a seaman's jacket and cap. "Run up there and get some help. I'll find my engineer and steam out to the wreck."

I ran down the road a little way and then doubled back to the skiff. When I was a few hundred yards out on the river, I stopped and waited because I wanted to make sure the ferryboat left on its rescue journey. It was a shame the widow wasn't there to see me, going to all this effort to save a gang of rapscallions. I had a feeling that she would have approved.

But all my work was wasted when I saw the wreck sliding down the river. The storm had lifted her off the rock and a cold shiver ran through me as I saw how low she was lying in the water. I rowed out to her but there was no sign of the gang. When I saw the ferryboat come up, I paddled away and watched as the captain circled around the wreck, calling out to her. Nobody answered his cries.

By the time I spotted Jim's lantern, the sun was coming up in the east, so we made for the nearest island. We hid the raft, sank the skiff and lay down to sleep like the dead.

LOOKING FOR CAIRO

After breakfast, we went through the gang's haul from the wreck – a great pile of boots, clothes, books and all kinds of swag. I stretched out on the bank and read stories to Jim about kings, dukes and queens and their fine gowns and golden crowns.

"I never knew there were so many of these royal people," Jim cried. "I've only heard of King Solomon. What kind of salary do they get, all these kings?"

"They can have what they want," I answered. "They own everything."

"That's the life," Jim chuckled. "And what do they do, Huck, to earn their money?"

"They just sit around. If there's a war on they might ride around rallying the troops. But most of the time they don't have to do anything."

"Sounds like a plumb job."

"Oh, it is," I said. "Well, that is unless the people get tired of the king. If they turn angry it can get downright dangerous. That King Louis in France lost his head."

"Lost it?"

"The people chopped it off. And they kept his little son, the *dolphin*, locked up in a prison until his dying day."

"The dolphin?" cried Jim.

"I'm sure he was called something like that."

"The poor boy," said Jim.

"Some people say he broke out of his cell and reached America. They say he's still here."

"But we don't have any kings in America," Jim replied. "What's he going to do for work?"

"He could teach people how to talk French."

"Don't they talk the same way we do?" cried Jim.

"You couldn't understand a word of it," I told him. "Not a single word."

"Amazing," he sighed. "And how did that happen?"

"I don't know, but it's true. I've seen some of it written in a book and it's mighty strange. What would you think if a man came up to you and said: "*Parlez-vous français?*"

"I wouldn't think twice about it," answered Jim. "I'd slap him on the side of the head.

"It's not an insult, Jim," I explained. "It's just asking if you speak French."

"Then why doesn't he say what he means?" said Jim.

"That's just how they talk in France."

"Craziness, that's what I call it. If we all spoke the same way it would be much easier, this life. I've got nothing else to say on the subject."

So I left it at that.

Our raft had been drifting south for weeks, and although we couldn't be sure of our exact position we thought another three nights on the water would bring us to the town of Cairo – where the Ohio River joined the great Mississippi. In Cairo, we planned to sell the raft and buy passage up the Ohio on a steamboat. This was the route to the 'Free States' where there was no slavery: Jim would be free and I'd be far away from the clutches of Pap or the widow.

On the second night a thick fog came down over the river and we decided to tie up until it cleared. I paddled to an island in my old canoe, dragging a line from the raft. But I couldn't find a grown tree to tie it to and, before I knew it, the current had carried the raft away and I was alone in the fog.

I paddled after Jim, but I could only see a few yards in any direction – the fog was as thick as wool. Away in the distance I heard a *whoop* and I chased after it. For ten minutes or more I went paddling after Jim's calls, whooping occasionally myself, until I didn't know if the raft was ahead or behind. The whoops got fainter and there was nothing to do but sit and wait while the fog closed around me, thicker than ever. It was cold and ghostly on the water and I was terrified that any second I might run straight into an island or a rocky bank.

Despite my fear in the swirling fog, I must have fallen asleep for several hours. When I opened my eyes I could see the stars glittering above the wide river. There was a speck on the water ahead of me and I paddled to reach it – it was the raft. Jim was sitting with his head between his knees, fast asleep, his right arm hanging over the steering oar. The raft was covered in torn branches, leaves and dirt. He'd had a rough time in the fog.

I tied up the canoe and decided to play a joke on my sleeping friend. "Hey Jim," I called, stretching my arms and yawning. "Have I been snoozing?"

"Why Huck," he cried, lifting his head, "is that really you? Let me look at you. Are you alive? It's too good to be true. I was sure you must be drowned and dead, out there in the fog."

"What's the matter with you?" I answered, pretending to be surprised. "Have you been drinking?"

"No, Huck," he protested, looking puzzled and a little hurt.

"Then why are you talking so wild?" I asked him. "Jim, I haven't been anywhere except right here."

He shook his head in disbelief. "It can't be," he cried. "Don't you remember going out in the canoe?"

"Going out where?"

"In all that fog?"

"What fog?" I shouted, trying to keep the joke going as long as I could. "I didn't see any fog. You've been dreaming, Jim, that's all it is, and you must have had a nightmare."

"But I nearly died," said Jim. "I was fighting the river most of the night. And when I saw you I almost cried in happiness."

"It was only a dream, Jim," I told him, firmly.

He closed his eyes and didn't say anything for five minutes. "Was it really a dream?" he finally muttered to himself. Then he looked down at the raft and he noticed all the dirt and the branches littered about everywhere.

"My heart broke when I thought you were gone," he

said slowly, meeting my eyes. "I didn't care what happened to me or the raft. When I woke up and saw you standing there, the tears welled up in my eyes. I could have got down on my knees to kiss your feet to show how grateful I was. And all you were thinking about was how to trick me and make me look like a fool."

He got up without saying another word and walked across to our wigwam. I couldn't believe I'd done anything so mean. It took me fifteen minutes to work myself up to go and apologize to a slave – but I did it and I was never sorry for it later. That was the last time I played a vicious trick on my friend Jim.

We were fast asleep for most of that day and only started out in the evening, following after a long raft that was carrying thirty men or more. She had five wigwams, two flagpoles and a campfire blazing in the middle. That was a river raft to be proud of.

When it got dark we kept a lookout for any lights or other sign of a town on the banks. The river was a mile wide here and I was worried that we might drift past Cairo and the entrance to the Ohio. Jim had better reasons than I did to be anxious.

"There she is," he cried, jumping up when he saw some lights. "There's my pathway to freedom."

But it was only a cloud of fireflies, away in the distance.

"Where is it, Huck?" he asked, trembling with excitement. "Where's that river? I've been a slave all my life, born in chains, Huck, but tomorrow I'll be free. You can't know how that makes a man feel."

Listening to Jim talk, I was suddenly overcome with guilt and a feeling of wretchedness. Here I was, helping a runaway slave to escape from his lawful owner – poor Miss Watson. This lady had gone out of her way to help me and how did I repay her kindness? I was taking Jim to the Free States and robbing her of eight hundred dollars. These thoughts made me feel so mean and miserable, I couldn't sit still. I began pacing up and down the raft with my guilty conscience goading me at every step.

"As soon as I get my freedom," Jim called over to me, "I'm going to save some money and buy my wife out of slavery. You know she's living on a farm not far from St. Petersburg? Well, we've got two children, Huck, and if I can't buy their freedom, I'll hire an Abolitionist to go down there and help them escape."

I shuddered when I heard Jim making his plans and talking so brazenly about those anti-slavers, the Abolitionists. It was bad enough that I was helping him to escape – but I wouldn't be responsible for other slaves being stolen from their masters. My heart set like stone and I decided to report him as a runaway the first chance I got. All at once, my mind was completely at rest.

"I see a light," Jim cried suddenly. "Over there, do you see it, Huck?"

"Yes, I do," I replied calmly. "Let me paddle over there in the canoe and see if it's safe to land."

Jim gave me a shove and clapped his hands together. "Oh Huck," he cried, "you're the best friend I ever had – and the only friend I've got now. I'd never have made it without you, Huck."

I felt sick when I heard him talking like that, but my conscience still told me I had to turn him in.

"You're my true friend," Jim called to me when the raft was some way off. "You've kept your promise, Huck, right from the beginning."

Well, I was crushed when I heard those words – and more confused than ever. But before I could make up my mind what to do, I heard a man shouting: "What's that over there? Who's there?"

Two men with guns were rowing in my direction in a small boat.

"It's a raft, sir," I answered quickly.

"Any people on it?" snapped one of the men.

"Just one," I replied.

"Five slaves ran off tonight," the man barked. "And we're chasing after them. Is that man on your raft black or white?"

I tried to say it, to tell them that Jim was a runaway slave. But the words wouldn't come. I just wasn't man enough to do it. "He's white, sir," I said finally.

"I reckon we'll see for ourselves," the man told me, and he took one end of my canoe while the other fellow started rowing in the direction of the raft.

"Oh, I wish you would come," I said quickly. "It's my pap and he needs a doctor. Perhaps you could tow us to shore? Pap's too weak to work the oars in his condition."

"What's the matter with him?" the man at the front asked.

"It's the...a...well, nothing much. Just a cold."

The man at the back stopped rowing. "Let go of that canoe," he whispered to his friend. "I reckon there's a case of smallpox on that raft."

"Don't leave us, sir," I pleaded. "I didn't tell you it was the pox because I was scared you'd abandon us. We've been stranded on the river for days."

"I feel sorry for you, son," the man at the front replied. "But we don't want the smallpox, you understand."

"That's what everyone says," I wailed. "Nobody wants to help."

"Those lights you can see on the shore are only a woodshed," the man told me. "But there's a town twenty miles downriver. They'll spot you in the daylight

and you can call them over. Say your father's got a fever and don't mention the pox. They'll get you and your pap to a doctor. And take this for the bill."

He took a twenty-dollar gold coin from his purse and the other man matched it with one from his own.

"Here," he said, "I'm sorry son, but it's the best we can do."

They rowed off into the night, hunting for runaway slaves, while I paddled back to the raft, feeling low-down and mean that I'd failed to do my duty and tell on Jim.

Forty dollars was a lot of money, enough to buy the tickets to the Free States and keep us fed and watered once we got there. Jim said we'd reach Cairo the following night and, sure enough, we saw lights flickering along the bank that evening. But, when I paddled out to a man in a nearby rowing boat, he laughed when I asked him if we'd arrived at Cairo. "You must be a halfwit, boy," he drawled. "Now stop bothering me and get along."

Jim said we'd find the town in the morning, but when the sun came up we noticed a new current of clear water running alongside the muddy Mississippi water. The two rivers were merging together. This could only mean that we'd already passed their meeting place at Cairo.

"It was the fog," whispered Jim. "We went by it in the fog."

There was nothing to do but wait until it was dark and try paddling back upstream in the canoe. We spent the afternoon dozing in the wigwam, but when we went to check the canoe it was gone, snatched away by the current. Jim said there was some bad magic working against us and I had to agree with him. We decided to continue our journey downstream on the raft and try to buy a canoe from some rafters or at a town. But the bad luck magic was still working against us.

We set out in the dark with the lantern swaying at the front of the raft. Around midnight I heard a steamboat pounding upriver. It was too dark to spot her until she was quite close, but when we did make her out I realized she was aiming straight for us. She was a big one, chugging through the water like a great, black cloud covered in tiny lights. I heard a shout and a bell ringing, then her monstrous bows were looming over us. Flames jumped from her furnace doors and the spray whistled around my ears. I went overboard on one side and Jim the other, as the mighty steamboat smashed into our little raft.

I swam for the bottom, knowing that a thirty-foot paddle wheel was about to sweep over my head if I didn't get out of the way. When my lungs were bursting for air, I broke the surface and was swamped by the steamboat's waves. She hadn't waited to pick up any survivors and was already vanishing from sight a mile upriver. Steamboat captains never did care much for rafters.

I hung around, shouting for Jim, but there was no sign of him. After ten minutes, I was so tired I clung onto a piece of driftwood and started kicking for the shore. I landed and dragged myself into some woods, staggering along until I came to a big log house. My plan was to creep past it, but the guard dogs must have heard me breathing. Before I could move another step they were snarling all around me.

BLOOD FEUD

"Who's out there?" a voice called from the house.

"George Jackson," I answered, giving the first name to spring into my head.

"What do you want here, George?"

"Nothing, sir," I replied. "I fell overboard off the steamboat."

"Strike a light there," ordered the voice. "Bring the guns. Are you alone, George?"

"Yes, sir."

"And do you know the Shepherdsons?"

"No, sir."

"Step forward, slowly," said the voice. "Come up to the door and squeeze yourself through."

I walked right up to the big, oak door at the front of the house. As I got closer I could hear locks and bars and bolts clicking open.

"Put your head through first," said the voice.

There was a candle on the floor and I could see three handsome men pointing guns at me. Waiting behind them in the gloom were three women.

"He looks safe enough," said one of the men, the father of the other two I reckoned, by the look of his silvery hair. "Come through to the sitting room."

They gathered around me, still holding their guns ready, and lifted a candle up to my face. "There isn't a trace of the Shepherdsons in his features," said one of the younger men.

"Young boy," said the elderly man kindly, "would you object to me searching you for weapons?"

"Not at all," I replied.

He patted my clothes to make sure I was unarmed and then nodded in satisfaction. "Let's hear your story," he asked with a smile.

"Wait one minute," the ladies interrupted. "Can't you see this boy's exhausted? He needs dry clothes and something to eat. Where's Buck? Buck!"

A young boy about the same age as me rushed in. "Now Buck," said one of the ladies, "take this boy up to your room and give him some clothes. We'll fix you some dinner in the meantime, Mr. Jackson, and then you can bed down in Buck's room. We'll hear your story in the morning, when you've had a chance to rest."

It was a fine family I'd happened across in those woods, and a fine old house. I'd never seen a better log house out in the country, with brass door handles, pictures on the walls, rugs or carpets in every room and a beautiful old clock on the mantelpiece.

Colonel Grangerford was the head of the family and a true gentleman. He and his wife accepted the cock and bull story I made up about being a poor orphan who'd fallen from the steamboat. They said I was welcome to stay in their house for as long as I wanted. The colonel was *well born*, as the saying goes, and that's worth as much in a man as it is a horse. Pap always told me that, even though he was no more 'well born' than a catfish.

The two elder sons were Tom and Bob and they were as handsome and well built as their father. All three men wore panama hats and linen suits so bright and white it hurt your eyes to look at them. There were two daughters, Sophia and Charlotte, and then Buck – the youngest child. He told me there had been three other sons and a daughter, but all of them had died.

The colonel owned dozens of farms and had over one hundred slaves on his properties. There were no other families in the district as rich and well born as his – except for the Shepherdsons. These two aristocratic families shared a steamboat landing and, as the weeks went by, I often saw the Shepherdsons riding along the roads on their fine horses.

I was out in the woods one day with Buck, when we heard a horseman coming. "Quick," cried Buck, "get behind this bush."

We peeked out through the leaves and I saw a young man riding in our direction along the track. It was Harney Shepherdson, one of the gentlemen I'd met at the landing. The next instant, Buck's gun exploded next to my ear and Harney's hat flew off his head. He grabbed a pistol and charged after us, but the trees were thick in this part of the woods and we reached the Grangerford log house safely.

The old colonel's eyes sparkled with delight when Buck told him the story. But then he frowned. "I don't like you hiding behind bushes," he said. "Step out into the road to do your shooting."

The moment I was alone with Buck I asked him if he'd wanted to kill the rider.

"Of course I did," he answered, with a grin.

"But why?" I said. "What's he ever done to you?"

"Nothing," Buck replied. "It's because of the feud."

"What's a *feud*?"

"Boy, you are ignorant," laughed Buck. "A feud is when two families quarrel and get to shooting and killing each other and it goes on for years and years and nobody's quite sure why it all started in the first

64

place. But you can't stop it. We've had two killings already this year, Huck, and they won't be the last, you can be sure of that."

I couldn't understand this feud business so the very next day I went down to the river for some peace and quiet, to get it straight in my head. Before I could sit down, one of the slaves from the house ran up and said he had something to show me over in a swamp. My curiosity was roused so I followed him deep into the woods.

"You step through there," he suggested at last, pointing to a thick bunch of trees and bushes. "You'll find something that might interest you."

He didn't wait for an answer, but went running through the woods back to the house. I did as he'd instructed and walked into a small clearing in the trees, as big as a bedroom in a house. There was a man sleeping in the middle of the clearing – my old friend Jim.

I woke him up, thinking he'd be astonished and delighted to see me standing there. He smiled and shook my hand, but he didn't seem at all surprised.

"I've been here all the time, Huck," he explained. "I followed you out of the water the night we were sunk."

"Why didn't you answer my shouts?" I asked him.

"What, and get caught as a runaway slave if some marshal stopped to help us? No, Huck, I had to be careful. I was going to stop you in the woods but the dogs got to you first. In the morning I met some of the slaves on the farm and they hid me away and brought me food. I've been keeping an eye on you ever since."

"Why didn't you send for me sooner?" I asked him.

"I was getting the raft ready," he replied.

"What raft?"

"Our old raft. One end of her was torn up a bit but she still floats alright. I found her caught on the banks and tied her up. But we lost all our supplies, Huck, so I've been collecting what we need."

"I can hardly believe it," I gasped.

"We'll be ready to go in a day or two," he grinned. "Back on the water."

I don't want to talk much about the next day, so I'll keep it short. At first light I woke up and noticed that Buck's bed was empty. When I slipped downstairs there was nobody around and the house was as quiet as a grave. One of the slaves was out in the front yard so I asked him where everyone was.

"Don't you know?" he whispered in amazement. "Miss Sophia ran off with Harney Shepherdson in the dead of the night. When the colonel found out, he rode off to the ferry landing with the boys, hoping to catch her."

I started running up the river road and soon I could hear guns blasting in the woods ahead. When I reached the landing, I stopped and climbed a tree by a woodpile, to get a clear view of what was happening. Several men on horses were charging around in front of the ferry. They were trying to drive out two boys who were hiding behind a stack of logs. One of the boys suddenly jumped up and shot a man out of his saddle. In the confusion, the boys ran toward my tree and sheltered behind the woodpile. One of the boys was Buck.

As soon as the men rode away with their injured friend, I called down from the tree. "Buck, where's your father?"

At first, Buck was so amazed to hear my voice he couldn't speak, but then he spotted me up in the tree.

"He's dead," Buck howled. "And my two brothers.

But I'll get even, don't you worry. I'll make the Shepherdsons pay for what they've done today." Before I could answer, shots rang out from the woods behind me. It was the same men who'd ridden away only a minute before. They'd doubled around to catch Buck and his friend with their backs against the woodpile.

The boys ran to the river, bleeding and hurt. I watched the men chase after them, shooting from the bank and shouting, "Kill them, kill them." It made me so sick I almost fell out of the tree. I can't speak about everything that took place after that – but I've seen it played out a thousand times in my nightmares.

When it got dark I climbed down and dragged the bodies from the shallows. I covered them up as best as I could, then went to find Jim. All I wanted was to get back on the wide river and leave that blood feud far behind.

MEETING ROYALTY

We floated along in the nights, stargazing, swimming in the cool water and enjoying the river's silence. One morning, I found a canoe and paddled to the shore, thinking I could pick some berries for our breakfast. Just as I was approaching the bank I saw two men running as if their lives depended on it. They came straight for me, shouting: "Stranger, save our lives. We're innocent men but they've set the dogs on us." I told them to splash around in the water a bit to throw off the scent, then they climbed aboard and I rowed them out to the raft.

One of the men must have been seventy or more. He had a bald head and white whiskers. The other fellow was about thirty. Their clothes were nothing fancy and their only possessions were a couple of ratty old carpet bags that looked as though they'd seen a lot of road in their time.

"What got you into trouble?" the old baldhead said to the other fellow, lounging in the canoe.

"Don't you know each other?" I asked in surprise.

"We just got acquainted on the outskirts of town," said the younger man. "I was leaving in a hurry, after hearing some complaints regarding a tooth-cleaning lotion I've been selling. It seems my lotion was stripping the enamel off my customers' choppers."

"And I was taking five dollars a night," the older man announced proudly, "giving speeches attacking the evils of drink. But word got around that I kept a jug of whiskey in my room. An unruly mob gathered at dawn, scheming to tar and feather me before running me out of town. I didn't linger for my breakfast."

"Old man, we could be partners for a while," the young fellow suggested.

"What exactly is your line of business?" the bald man asked.

"Anything and everything, as long as there's no work involved in it. How about you?"

"Oh, preaching and doctoring mainly, but I'm always interested in learning new ways to take a dollar off a sucker without getting caught."

We were all silent for a moment, while I kept rowing steadily across the river.

"Oh, alas," cried the young fellow, suddenly.

"What are you *alassing* about?" muttered the older man, suspiciously.

"To think my sad and pitiful life has led me to this, dragged down into such company." He picked up a rag and wiped his eye.

"Is our company not good enough for you?" cried the old man, clearly offended.

"It's all I deserve," replied the younger man. "But if you knew my secret, you'd understand."

"What secret is that?" I asked him.

"The secret of my birth," he replied mysteriously.

"Gentlemen, I will reveal everything to you. By rights, I am a duke!"

"You can't mean it?" cried the old man.

"But it's true," said the duke. "My grandfather was the Duke of Bridgewater. Following a long and tangled chain of events, my own father came to America and his dukedom was stolen from him. I am the rightful Duke of Bridgewater, but just look at me – hunted, dressed in rags and degraded to the fellowship of felons on a crude river raft."

We had reached the raft and Jim and I stood with our mouths hanging open in amazement as we listened to this speech.

"My friends," the duke continued, "it would ease my pain slightly if you would address me as 'Your Grace' or 'Your Lordship' when you serve me dinner. My heart is broken, but if you could make a little bow before you speak, and treat me with the respect a duke deserves, I would be thankful."

Jim and I said we'd try to follow his instructions as best we could, but the old man looked uncomfortable with the arrangement. He shuffled around the raft all through the morning, grumbling to himself and rubbing his chin. At last he cried out: "Look, Bilgewater, you're not the only man on this raft with a dazzling secret."

To our amazement, he began to weep.

"Bilgewater," he sobbed, "can I trust you with the truth of my origins?"

"To the death," replied the duke.

"I am the *Dauphin*," the old man shouted.

"It's the dolphin," cried Jim.

"But you're so old," gasped the duke. "By rights, the dauphin should only be in his fifties."

"Trouble and pain have done it," howled the old man. "I've grown old before my time. You see before you the rightful King of France."

Jim and I tried to comfort the king as much as we could, but he wouldn't stop his moaning and crying.

"Do one thing for me, gentlemen," he asked between sobs. "Call me 'Your Majesty' when you bow down to me."

The duke looked pretty sour when he heard the king giving his orders. But the king stuck his hand out as a peace offering: "No hard feelings, Duke," he said. "A raft's too small for festering arguments." And they shook hands, warily.

It didn't take long for me to realize that these two liars weren't kings or dukes, just low-down frauds and tricksters. But I never said anything about it. I had no objections to flattering them, as long as I had an easy life. It's always best not to make trouble, if you can possibly avoid it.

When they asked about Jim, I made up a story about him being my slave. I told them my father and I had been bound for New Orleans, but he had been drowned the night we ran into the steamboat.

"We can't run the raft in the daylight," I sighed, "because men keep coming out and asking if Jim's a runaway. I'm tired of explaining it."

The duke said he'd come up with some scheme that would allow us to travel the river in the day, without disturbance. Then the royals moved their things into the wigwam, and laid their heads down to sleep.

EASY MONEY

Rising late in the morning, the king and duke played cards for an hour or two, before they set to work plotting and planning their 'campaign of action' as they called it.

"Some of the best scams I've ever seen were theatrical shows," the duke began. "Did you ever 'tread the boards' Your Majesty?"

"Never," replied the king.

The duke rummaged around in his carpetbag and brought out a fistful of crumpled posters. "The first good town we come to, we'll stage a show," he announced. "Let me see," he mumbled, leafing through the posters. "Aha," he cried, holding up a greasy example, "we'll do some Shakespeare. Are you willing to learn the necessary words, King?"

"Always," replied the king.

Before long they were prancing and acting all around the raft, waving sticks in the air for swords and shouting out brave words and speeches. I'd never seen a stranger thing in all my life. The duke even had some ragged old stage costumes in his bag.

"It'll be a sure-fire hit," he declared when both men were exhausted. "Now, Huck," he said, waving me over. "There's a one-horse town around this bend. If we stop there, I should be able to fix things for you and your slave."

We needed coffee and other supplies, so I went into town with the two rascals while Jim guarded the raft. The streets and houses were deserted and the only inhabitant we could find was a sick slave resting on a rocking chair.

"There's a camp meeting, two miles back in the woods," he told us. "Everyone's gone to hear the preachers."

"Preachers?" said the king. "That sounds like my kind of business."

I said I'd tag along with him if he didn't mind the company, but the duke wanted to stay in town. "I'm looking for a printing shop," he chuckled, with a wink. "See you back at the raft."

There were over a thousand people at that religious gathering and the woods were full of carts and wagons, with teams of horses and oxen flicking their tails in the shade of the trees. Crowds milled around a little village of tents selling watermelons, lemonade and gingerbread. But the king didn't stop for refreshments. He hurried straight over to a large tent where a preacher was giving a sermon to a great throng of people. The preacher shook his fists in the air and called down fire and lightning on the world's sinners. He told anyone who wanted forgiveness to make his or her way to the mourner's bench at the front of the stage. Women were screaming and tearing at their hair and grown men wept like babies as they heard him talk.

The next thing I knew, the king was wailing and groaning louder than anyone in the tent. He beat his chest and raced up to the stage, begging a chance to talk to the crowd. The preacher welcomed him onto the podium and the king began by saying he was a pirate – a real pirate from the Indian Ocean. He said he'd lost most of his crew in a deadly sword fight and had come back to New Orleans to recruit new pirates. But, he'd been robbed and thrown from a steamboat before he could reach the city. The experience had changed him forever. All he desired now was to return to the Indian Ocean and begin the task of reforming every pirate he came across.

The crowd roared louder than ever when they heard this story. "Take up a collection to save the pirates," a lady next to me screamed. "No. Let the reformed pirate take the collection," called another man.

I watched, dumbstruck, as the king weaved through the ranks of people, collecting coins and notes from a hundred pairs of outstretched hands.

"To the raft, Huck," he wheezed, when he finally reached me at the edge of the tent. We didn't waste any time getting back to the river. Later that afternoon I watched the king counting out a haul of eighty-seven dollars from his battered old hat.

The duke had his own surprise for us, though he couldn't match the royal sum of money raised by the king. Finding the printer's shop empty and the door unlocked, he'd helped himself to the press and printing materials.

Standing proudly in the middle of the raft, he unrolled a large 'WANTED' poster he'd made, with a drawing of a runaway slave and some paragraphs of text that described Jim in every detail.

"If someone stops us during the daytime," he explained, "we can show them this poster and say we're taking Jim back to his plantation to claim the reward."

We all agreed the duke was a real smart schemer, and I pushed the raft away from the shore. But when Jim called me to take my watch at four o'clock in the morning, he looked worried. "Huck," he whispered, "are we going to run across any more kings or dukes on this trip?"

"I reckon not," I answered.

"That's good," he sighed with relief. "I don't mind one or two of them, but that's enough. Those royals in our wigwam are dead drunk."

Jim told me that he'd asked the king to speak some French, so he could hear what it sounded like. But that old rascal said he'd been in America so long he'd forgotten every word of it.

The two royals looked pretty groggy when they stumbled out of the wigwam the next morning. But, after they'd been for a swim and eaten some breakfast, they were ready to get back to their theatrical rehearsing. The king jumped up and started calling out a speech: "Romeo, Romeo," he boomed. "Where on earth are you, Romeo?"

"No, no," the duke scolded him. "You're supposed to be a young, sensitive girl in that scene. Don't bray like a donkey. Let's try that sword fight again."

They took up their sticks and the next second they were hopping around the raft, stabbing at each other. It was all very convincing until the king tripped and tumbled into the river. After that the two actors rested in the shade of the wigwam, talking in whispers. From time to time I heard the duke raise his voice in excitement: "For my encore," he cried, "I shall perform a speech that will leave them weeping in their seats."

"How does it go?" coughed the king.

"To be or not to be," said the duke slowly, "that is the bare bodkin." And he went on like that for twenty minutes or more, weeping and wailing over every word. None of us on the raft could understand what he was talking about. He recited it over and over for days, teaching it to the king, but it always brought a tear to my eye when I heard it. Nobody could get down to that acting business quite like the duke.

We had drifted downriver into the state of Arkansas when the duke and king informed me that their show was finally ready. Spying a little town, Jim hid the raft in a grove of cypress trees, while the rest of us paddled over there in the canoe.

By a piece of luck there was a circus in town that day and all the country people were flooding in to buy their tickets. The duke hired a stage in the courthouse and we went around sticking up the posters he'd fished out of his carpetbag. They promised:

AN INCREDIBLE, UNFORGETTABLE, ONCE IN A LIFETIME EXPERIENCE

I didn't doubt that claim for one second.

In the afternoon I went over to the circus and waited until the watchman passed by before diving under the tent. I had my twenty dollars in gold and some other money, but I thought it would be safer to hang onto it, rather than waste it buying a ticket. There's no telling when you'll need money, when you're among strangers and a long way from home.

It was a wonderful circus. There were dozens of riders and all the ladies looked like queens, dressed in clothes that cost millions of dollars and covered with diamonds and other jewels. I don't think I've ever seen a lovelier sight.

The riders did the most astonishing tricks and there was a clown running around who got the whole crowd laughing. Everyone was rolling around on the benches enjoying the show when, suddenly, a drunkard ran into the ring and started shouting that he wanted to go for a ride on one of the horses. The ringmaster tried to throw him out, but the drunkard wouldn't leave and the whole circus came to a standstill.

"Get rid of him," a lady screamed, and the crowd started booing at the drunkard. But the ringmaster lifted his hands and made a little speech. He said that he'd give the man what he wanted and then they could get on with the performance. Two circus hands came over leading a wild-looking stallion and the drunkard climbed up to the saddle on his back, rolling and reeling with his feet in the stirrups. The horse snorted and charged off and my heart skipped a beat. It looked certain that the man would be thrown off and killed, but somehow he clung on.

Then I watched, amazed, as he dragged his legs up and stood up tall and proud on the horse's back. He began stripping his clothes away and throwing them into the audience, while the horse never stopped its charge around the tent. When he tore off the last layer of his rough old clothes I saw that he was wearing a circus outfit. He jumped down from the horse and took a bow, while the crowd howled with pleasure and astonishment. It was the best circus I'd ever seen.

That same night we had our own show at the courthouse, but only twelve people came to see it. They laughed in all the wrong places and left before the end, except for one boy who fell asleep at the back of the room. When the duke stepped down from the stage he was spitting mad. "These Arkansas lunkheads," he snarled. "Shakespeare's too good for them."

The next morning the duke rushed around town with a pot of black paint and an artist's brush. He crossed out the old posters for the show and added:

ALL NEW SHOW AT THE COURTHOUSE
TONIGHT
NO LADIES NOR CHILDREN ADMITTED

"That should do it," he declared. "If that doesn't bring the crowds rushing in, I don't know Arkansas."

That night the house was jam-packed with men in no time at all. We had to turn people away. The duke came onto the stage with the curtain down behind him. He made a speech, bragging about the thrilling theatrical experience that awaited the audience. When he had everyone warmed up and feverish with excitement, he raised the curtain and the king came bounding out wearing the strangest costume I'd ever seen. He was painted like a rainbow, streaked and striped on every part of his almost naked body. The audience almost died laughing when they saw that old fool prancing around the stage in such a funny outfit. When he ducked behind the curtain, they called him out for another look. Each time he left the stage they yelled for him to return.

Then the duke dropped the curtain and made an announcement. He said the show was over but it would run for two more nights before 'pressing engagements' forced the company to leave town.

Every man there shouted: "Is that all there is?" A moment later they were rushing for the stage and waving their fists in the air. "Give us our money back, you crooks," one fellow demanded.

"Boys, boys, wait a minute," called a well-dressed man, climbing onto the stage. "We've been cheated, I know. But do you want to be the laughing stock of the whole town? What we need to do is leave quietly and tell all our friends how *good* the show is. Then they'll come along and be swindled too and we'll all be in the same boat."

The men nodded and grumbled their approval. Sure enough, the following evening we had a full house of newcomers and cheated them the same way. But, on the third night, I could see that the crowd was made up of people who'd already attended the show. I couldn't help noticing that their coats and pockets were bulging, and I thought there was a funny smell of bad eggs and cabbages wafting through the hall.

The duke closed the ticket office when the place was full, then set out for the stage door with me following. But as soon as we turned a corner he whispered: "Walk fast until you get past the houses, then run for that raft like the dogs are after you."

We arrived at the river puffing for breath. Ten seconds later, Jim was shoving us off from the banks. The king stuck his head out of the wigwam and asked sleepily: "Hello boys, how was the take?" He hadn't even been in town that evening.

"We had a full house," the duke chuckled. "I knew those greenhorns would send their friends to see the show on the second night, then come for their revenge on the third. But they won't get any. They can have a picnic for all I care – they brought plenty of provisions for one."

Those rascals had raised four hundred and sixty-five dollars in ticket money. When they were asleep and snoring, Jim came over to see me.

"Doesn't it surprise you sometimes, Huck," he asked, "the way the king and the duke carry on?"

"No, it doesn't," I replied.

"But they're no better than a pair of rapscallions," whispered Jim. "Frauds and cheats."

"I know, but I reckon all royalty behaves like that, Jim. I've read about them in the history books and you wouldn't believe some of the things they get up to. I wish I knew of a country that didn't have any royalty, but I don't. So, until I do, we've got to put up with them as best we can."

TWO BROTHERS

At the next town we came to the duke and the king bought themselves elegant new clothes. I hardly recognized the king when he popped out of the wigwam in his coal-black suit and hat. One moment he was a ragged old river rat in torn jeans and a baggy checked shirt, the next he looked like a wealthy banker stepping out of his city office.

Ten miles downriver we saw a steamboat moored close to the bank, taking on freight. There was a small town a mile or two further on and the king said he'd like to ride down to it on the steamboat and pretend he was a big shot coming in from the north.

"Making a grand entrance can be good for business, Huckleberry," he chuckled.

He asked me to accompany him as his manservant. I didn't need any persuading: riding on a steamboat was a special treat for any boy. So, I jumped into the canoe and paddled him to the shore. When we were still some distance from the steamboat, the king saw a man with a carpetbag, resting on the bank. He hailed him: "Where are you bound for, sir?"

"Down to the steamboat," replied the man.

"Get aboard," called the king. "Wait, my servant,

Adolphus, will help you with your bags."

I jumped out and grabbed the carpetbag, then the three of us set off in the canoe.

"Where've you come from?" asked the man.

"St. Louis," replied the king in a sugary voice. "I'm staying with a friend not far from here.

"Oh," said the man. "I thought you might have been Mr. Wilks, arriving only a day too late."

"Late for what?" purred the king.

"His poor brother, Peter, died yesterday," the man explained. "For the last three weeks Peter's been talking about nothing else but seeing his long-lost brothers from England, Harvey and William. Harvey's old like you, begging your pardon sir, but William's only in his thirties. He's deaf and dumb, they say. And nobody's set eyes on either of them for twenty years or more."

"Didn't anybody write with the news?" asked the king.

"They sent a letter a month or two ago but there's been no reply. It's a terrible shame. Peter didn't leave any will, you see. But he's been swapping letters with his brothers for years and has left everything to Harvey, trusting him to make arrangements for the girls."

"Did you say you were going to New Orleans?" the king said craftily.

"I'm going further than that, sir," answered the man, boldly. "Brazil is my final destination."

"And how many Wilks girls are there?"

"Three teenagers, sir. Mary Jane, Susan and Joanna. Mary Jane is a beauty."

"I see," said the king. "Tell me some more about this fellow, Peter."

The old man asked so many questions our passenger almost went hoarse. He asked about everyone in the town, what they did for a living, how old they were and how well they knew the dead man. Finally, he said slyly: "Was Peter Wilks a wealthy man?"

"Oh yes, sir," cried the man. "People say he had a fortune of thousands of dollars in gold."

"His funeral will be tomorrow, I suppose," said the king and the man nodded sadly. "It's a depressing business, and that's a fact," the king continued. "But we've all got to go, one day or another."

We had reached the steamboat but, instead of going aboard for our ride, the king shook the young man's hand and waved him farewell.

"Turn our canoe around, Alphonsus," ordered the forgetful old fool, and we paddled away. As soon as we were out of earshot of the steamboat, he told me to hurry back to get the duke. "Let's hope Bilgewater knows how to act deaf and dumb," he hissed under his breath.

When the king had gone through the whole story with the duke, we set out to shore three miles above the town to hail another steamboat. It was the middle of the afternoon before we spotted a big one. The steamboat crew rowed us into town and a large group of men swarmed down the main street to greet us.

"Can any of you gentlemen direct me to the

house of Mr. Peter Wilks?" asked the king, in a fair English accent.

The men glanced at one another and nodded and winked.

"I'm sorry, sir," one of them replied. "You're too late."

Quick as a flash, the king's legs went all rubbery and he leaned against the fellow who had spoken. "Oh, this is hard news, sir," he moaned. "Too hard to bear."

Then he turned around, with the tears streaming down his face, and made a series of idiotic hand signals to the duke. The duke dropped his carpetbag and burst out crying too. Both those rascals sobbed for all they were worth. It was enough to make me feel ashamed of the human race.

The news was all over town in two minutes and you could see people running to us from every direction. Pretty soon we were in the middle of a big crowd and everyone started tramping up the main street in the direction of the Wilks' house. People poked their heads over fences and stood out in their yards just to get a good look at us.

"Is it really *them*?" I heard a lady call.

"You bet it is," came the answer.

When we got to the house, the street in front was packed and the three girls were standing on the porch. Mary Jane really was a beauty and her face and her eyes were lit up with happiness to see her long-lost uncles. The king spread his arms wide open and Mary Jane hugged him, while the other two girls grabbed the duke. Half the crowd started sobbing with joy when they saw the reunion and the other half were clapping and whooping.

The king looked around and saw the coffin, resting on two chairs at the side of the porch. He lifted one hand to the duke's shoulder and the two fraudsters stared down at the ground. Then they shuffled over to the dead man's box. Everybody dropped back to give them some breathing room and the talk and noise all stopped. The men in the crowd took off their hats and it got so quiet you could have heard a pin fall. When those impostors reached the coffin, they leaned over, took one look and started boo-hooing loud enough to be heard in New Orleans. They put their arms around each other and wept like a pair of newborn babies.

I'd never seen two men cry like that before. Next, they got down on their knees and rested their foreheads against the coffin wood, pressing their hands together in prayer. When the crowd saw this act of fake brotherly love they started weeping with all their might. Soon the whole street was damp with tears. The women lined up to hug and weep over the three girls, touching their brows and glancing up at the sky when they were finished. I had never seen anything so disgusting in all my life.

The king finally got to his feet and spoke to the crowd, punctuating every word with a sob. He said it was a terrible trial for the two brothers to have voyaged four thousand miles to visit their dear Peter and to miss him by just a single day. "But," he added, "the sympathy displayed and the holy tears shed by you sweet townspeople have made it easier to bear our burden." It made me feel sick to listen to him.

Someone in the crowd started up with a hymn and soon the whole crowd was singing. It reminded me of the camp gathering. After all that hogwash and rot from the king, I was glad to hear the music. It sounded clean and honest compared to his lies.

Then the king waved his arms for silence. "My brother and I," he said humbly, "would like to invite the dearest, closest friends of our brother Peter for an evening meal." He dropped a few names into the invitation, all taken from the lips of the fellow we had met on the river that morning. Some men and their wives stepped forward and shook the king's hand. They tried speaking to the duke, but he just smiled and made baby noises, pretending he didn't have the power of speech.

While the two fraudsters were shaking hands and

wiping their eyes, Mary Jane disappeared into the house and returned with the letter her father had written for Harvey. The king read it aloud to the crowd. Peter wanted the girls to have three thousand dollars when everything was sold, but the bulk of the estate was left to Harvey and William. The letter detailed the various buildings and business concerns the two rogues had inherited and went on to say there was six thousand dollars in gold buried in the cellar of the family house.

"William and I want everything to be open and above board," the king declared. "We'll bring the gold now and do a count."

He ordered me to bring a candle and we hurried down to the cellar. When they found the bag, those two crooks emptied its contents onto the floor. It was a lovely sight, all that glinting, gleaming gold.

"This beats the theatrical business, don't it, Bilgewater?" laughed the king.

"It surely does," murmured the duke, running his fingers through the pile of gold. "Let's count it up."

I would never have thought of counting the coins but it was a good thing they did. The pile was four hundred and fifteen dollars short of six thousand.

"He must have made a mistake," gasped the duke.

"The swine," snapped the king. "I was planning to show those greenhorns how honest we are by doing the count in front of their noses."

"We can make it up with our own money," suggested the duke. "We've got just enough to do it. Then we'll have the count and hand it over to the girls."

"To the girls?" cried the king. "Why, duke, that's a brilliant idea. Who'll suspect us then? We can steal it at our leisure."

Those rapscallions made a big show of stacking all the gold coins onto a little table, while all the townspeople greedily stared at the treasure and licked their lips. When they'd finished the count, the king raked it all into the bag. "My friends," he called to the crowd. "What kind of men would we be, to take this money from these poor little lambs?" He motioned to the three, weeping Wilks girls. "William and I have decided that it would be robbery, yes *robbery*, not to turn every cent of this money over to these needy sisters, immediately."

The next instant everybody was hugging and weeping and wailing with the same frenzied energy as before. It was a torment to watch it. But, just as the king launched into another of his slushy speeches, I noticed a square-jawed man pushing his way through the crowd. He was the only person there who wasn't crying or smiling. Instead, he was listening intently to the king's waffle. The king finally spotted him and then someone in the crowd shouted: "Here's Dr. Robinson. Step up, doctor, and meet the Wilks brothers."

The king rushed forward with his hand outstretched. But the man crossed his arms, rudely. "Keep your hands off me," he snapped. "That's the worst imitation of an English accent I've ever heard. You're a brazen fraud." He stepped straight over to Mary Jane. "I was your father's friend," he told her.

"I'm warning you now, Mary, turn your back on that scoundrel. He's an ignorant tramp who's picked up a few names and facts about our town somewhere and is trying to fleece you. Turn this rascal out, I beg you, as an honest friend. Will you do it?"

Mary Jane straightened herself up and said boldly: "Here is my answer."

She lifted the money bag from the table and handed it to the king.

"Please look after this gold for me and my sisters," she said proudly. "We don't need a receipt."

She put her arms around the king and the crowd clapped their hands and stomped on the floor to show their approval. It was so loud it sounded like a storm was breaking over us.

"Then I wash my hands of the matter," the doctor said crossly. "But I warn you, Mary Jane, the time will come when you'll feel sick thinking back on this day."

"All right, doctor," the king replied in a mocking voice. "And if it does, we can always send for you."

The crowd hooted and laughed at the king's jibe while the doctor hurried away.

GOLD FEVER

When the crowd thinned out and went home at last, the king asked Mary Jane if there were any spare rooms in the house.

"There is one small room which Uncle William may use," she replied sweetly, "and you may have my room, Uncle Harvey. I can move in with my sisters, and your servant will find a mattress in the attic."

She took us up to our rooms and said she could move her dresses out if the king needed more space. They were hanging behind a floor-length curtain at one end of her bedroom, but the king said there was no need to disturb them.

That evening they had a big supper for the duke and the king and I had to stand behind their chairs, waiting on them. It was a fine dinner, although I only tasted the leftovers in the kitchen. While I was helping myself to a plateful, the youngest girl, Joanna, ran in and started pumping me for gossip about England.

"Did you ever meet the king?" she asked with a giggle.

"All the time," I lied. "He comes to our church."

"What? Up in Sheffield?" she asked. "You mean he leaves his palace in London and travels hundreds of miles to go to church every Sunday?"

Of course, I had no idea which town I was supposed to live in, or how far it was from London. I was so stumped I had to pretend I was choking on a chicken bone to buy myself some time.

"Well, it is a long way," I told her, "but he always drops in to say hello when he's doing a tour of the country."

"That's a stretcher, I reckon," she cried. "And your accent's ever so funny. Tell me about Sheffield. I bet you don't know a thing about it."

I was reaching for another piece of chicken when Mary Jane suddenly stepped into the room and saved me. "Joanna," she said sternly, "are you being rude to our guest?"

"No, I wasn't," Joanna protested. "He told me a stretcher."

"It doesn't matter what he told you," Mary Jane explained. "What's important is always to respect our guests and treat them kindly. This poor boy is a long way from his home and family and we mustn't say cruel things that might upset him."

It broke my heart to think I was letting those two reptiles, the duke and the king, steal money from a girl as sweet as Mary Jane. Then Susan came into the room and when she heard the story she asked Joanna to apologize. I had to listen to Joanna make the sweetest apology I'd ever heard – and all the time I was feeling low-down and mean for my part in the fraudsters' deception. It was all too horrible to bear. I decided at once that I would steal the gold back for the girls – no matter what risks were involved.

The bedrooms were all empty and dark when I climbed upstairs. I stepped into the duke's room and started feeling around in the gloom with my hands, searching for the money bag. There was no trace of it, so I decided it must be hidden in the king's quarters. I sneaked into his room and was pawing around in a trunk of clothes when I heard footsteps out in the hall. There was no time to get out of the room, so I slipped behind the curtain that concealed Mary Jane's dresses and stood perfectly still.

"Well, what is it?" hissed the king, when they had shut the door behind them. "Make it snappy."

"I'm not comfortable," the duke whispered. "That doctor's making me feel uneasy about things. I think we should leave tonight and get downriver with the gold."

My heart sank when I heard his plan. If I'd acted sooner, I might have saved the gold for the girls.

"But all the property belongs to us," the king replied. "It's worth thousands of dollars and we can sell it before we scram."

"I don't like taking *everything* from the orphans," the duke grumbled. "The gold's good enough for me."

"Don't fret about those girls," the king whispered. "When we slip away, all the contracts of sale will be declared invalid. You can't sell something you don't own. They'll get it all back. Even the slaves."

"And what about the doctor?" asked the duke.

"We don't have to worry about him," the king replied scornfully. "We've got the whole town eating out of our hands. Try to keep your cool, duke, and we'll double our money and get away safely."

This argument convinced the duke it was worth staying, but just as they were leaving to go downstairs he tapped the king on the arm. "Wait," he whispered. "I don't think our money's safe behind that curtain. What if one of the slaves cleans up the room and finds it there? They're bound to help themselves to a few dollars."

"You're right," replied the king and I heard him step nearer to me and reach down to the floorboards by my feet. His hand fumbled under the curtain and snatched up the money bag. It was so close I had almost tripped over it.

"Let's stash it inside the mattress," suggested the duke. "Even if they make up the bed they won't look inside there. It's as safe as a bank in there."

I had the gold under my arm before they were

halfway downstairs. The best place to hide it would be somewhere outside the house, but I didn't want to leave when it was still dark. So, I hid the bag in my attic bedroom and waited nervously for dawn.

At first light, I could hear those rascals snoring in their rooms, so I tiptoed downstairs with the gold. I had planned to go through the dining room and out through the front doors, but they were still locked when I tried the handle. Before I could sneak back to the kitchen door, I heard someone on the stairs and ducked into a side room. I turned around and there was the open coffin and poor old Peter's remains staring up at me. There was nowhere else to hide the money but next to the dead man. I slipped the bag under the lid, shivering when I touched his ice-cold hands, and ran to get behind the door.

Mary Jane stepped into the room, kneeled by the coffin and began to cry. She had her back to me, so I tiptoed out of the room and ran back to the attic. Then I tossed and turned on my mattress, thinking how stupid I'd been to go charging around the house with six thousand dollars and no idea where to hide it. If the money was buried with Peter, I could write to Mary Jane when I got downriver and tell her the secret, but it was more likely that someone would find the gold when they went to screw down the coffin lid.

The house slowly came to life and I went downstairs for my breakfast. All through the morning I kept going to peek inside the coffin room, but there was always a mourner or an undertaker's man sitting in there. The lid looked as though it hadn't been moved so I thought the money was safe.

At midday, people began to flock in for the funeral. The undertaker slid around in black gloves, arranging the seats around the coffin. He was as quiet as a cat. The two crooks sat at the front of the room with the girls, while a long line of mourners started to file past the coffin. The room was soon jam-packed with townspeople in their best black clothes. The parson stood up to give his sermon. But, the moment he was on his feet, a dog started barking in the cellar. The dog got louder and louder until you couldn't hear a word of the sermon. I saw the undertaker give the parson a reassuring nod and go gliding out of the room to the cellar. We all heard a whack and a yelp from the dog and then there was silence. The undertaker slid back into the room and worked his way around the walls until he was finally back in his chair. "He had a rat," he whispered to the parson.

It was a good sermon, but too long and tiresome for my liking. When it was over, I watched the undertaker step over to the coffin and close the lid. He started screwing it shut and he never blinked, so I didn't think he'd noticed the gold.

But I had no way of knowing if the bag was still there *before* he closed the lid. Some rascal might have pinched it. What would Mary Jane think of me if I told her to raise her poor father's bones and it turned out there was no money in the box? I wished that I had never tried to save the gold in the first place. All I'd done was to make the whole business a hundred times more complicated.

They buried him and we came home. About an hour later, the king announced that he and William would soon be returning to England and they invited the girls to go with them, to start a new life in Sheffield. In the circumstances, he said, they had decided to sell the three slaves who had lived with the family most of their lives; a slave trader was coming that afternoon to collect them. The rest of the estate would be put up for auction the following day. When the Wilks girls heard the fate of their old friends, the tears streamed down their cheeks and they ran sobbing to their rooms. It was late in the evening before they finally came downstairs. They thanked the tricksters for their kindness and said how excited they were to be visiting England.

The king and the duke climbed up to my attic cubbyhole at first light, with faces black as thunder. "Have you been in my room, Huckleberry?" the king growled.

"No, Your Majesty," I replied. "Not since Mary Jane showed us around."

"Have you seen anyone go in there?" asked the duke. I only had a second to think but I saw my chance.

"Just the slaves," I told him.

"Which slaves?" the king cried.

"I saw two of the house slaves tiptoe out of there on the day of the funeral."

"On tiptoe, you say," whispered the duke. "Why didn't you warn us?"

"It wasn't unusual for them to tiptoe," I answered. "Perhaps they didn't want to make a noise in case you were sleeping?"

"That must be it," gasped the king, looking sick.

"And we sold them yesterday afternoon for a song," said the duke, with his eyes flaming. "They conned us good and proper, Your Majesty. They'll be halfway to Ohio by now, after buying themselves free."

"We've got to swallow it," snarled the king. "And not say a word."

"We wouldn't be swallowing anything if you'd listened to me," said the duke, with a sneer. "We'd be on the river with that gold."

"There's still the auction for the estate," snapped the king. "Keep your mouth shut, William, and we'll come out of this rich men."

I dawdled for an hour, dressing slowly as I waited for the two rascals to cool down. When I stepped onto the landing I saw Mary Jane sitting in her room, packing her things away in the trunk. She really thought she was going to England. I cleared my throat to let her know I was there, but she didn't turn around. I suddenly realized that she was crying and I stepped boldly into her room.

"Why the tears, Miss Mary Jane?" I asked her.

She explained that even though she knew the estate had to be sold, the slaves had been like family to her and she was heartbroken that she was never going to see them again.

"Oh, but you will see them," I blurted out, without thinking what I was saying. "And sooner than you think."

She jumped up and hugged me. "Is that true?" she cried.

"Every word of it," I replied.

"But how can you know? How can I trust you?"

I didn't say anything for a whole minute, while Mary Jane stared up at me with her puppy eyes and her lovely smile. My mind was racing, trying to decide between telling her the truth and getting out of it with a lie. I decided to risk the truth, throwing in a few precautions.

"Is there somewhere you can stay, out of town, for two or three nights?" I asked her.

"I have a friend I can visit," she replied. "Why?"

"If I tell you the truth, will you promise to trust me and to visit your friend?"

"Of course," she smiled.

"Then sit down and get ready for a shock. Just sit still and take it like a man – don't scream. Those men downstairs who say they're your uncles, well, they're frauds, liars, cheats and deadbeats. They're fake. That's the worst thing I have to tell you, Mary Jane. The rest isn't half as bad."

She looked up at me with her eyes blazing and I told her everything that had happened – from the first meeting with the man on his way to Brazil, to the tearful reunion on her front porch. Her face flamed as red as a sunset and she jumped off the bed. "Those brutes," she cried. "I'll make sure they're tarred and feathered and thrown into the river. There's not a second to waste."

"You made me a promise, Mary Jane," I reminded her.

"Forgive me," she sighed, falling back onto the bed. "I lost my temper for a moment. Now, tell me what I must do."

"Well," I said, "it's a rough gang we're dealing with, and I can't just run out on them. There's someone else I have to protect, you understand? He can't afford to get mixed up in all this." I was thinking of Jim, of course. If we were rounded up by the townspeople I could try to explain that I had nothing to do with the fraud, but Jim would be arrested at once as a runaway slave.

"But I've got a plan to get those crooks locked up," I told her in a whisper. "Once they're behind bars, I can slip away with my friend. Will you help me?"

"Any way I can," she replied in a brave voice.

"Then go out to your friend's house, as though you're staying the night," I told her in a whisper. "But slip back here before eleven o'clock. When you get back, put a candle in the window, so I know that you're at home, and wait until eleven. If I *don't* come it means I'm out of the way and safe. Then you can spread the news around about your uncles and get them jailed."

"I want you to be free of those criminals," said Mary Jane, "but if you're not here to speak against them, how can I prove they're liars?"

"Have you got a pen and paper I could use?" I asked her. Then I wrote down the name of the town where the king and the duke had conned the audience at the courthouse. "If they won't confess," I chuckled, "send a note to the sheriff of this town and ask him to come downriver to identify two conmen actors. I'm sure he'll be happy to oblige."

"But how can we stop the auction today?" she cried. "We'll lose all our property."

"You won't lose anything," I assured her. "The property and the slaves will be returned to you and all the money refunded to the buyers, as soon as the crooks are exposed."

"You've put my mind at rest," she said sweetly. "I'll have my breakfast and then I'll go straight to my friend Mr. Lothrop's house."

"But you have to go *before* breakfast," I cried. "Why do you think I want you out of the way? Those two fraudsters will be watching everyone like hawks. If they notice any change in you they'll be suspicious. Will you be able to give them a 'good morning' kiss without flinching?"

"You're right," she said, with a shudder. "I couldn't do it. I'll make some excuse to my sisters and leave at once. If Harvey asks where I am, you can tell him I'm saying goodbye to some of my old friends."

"There's one last thing I have to tell you," I whispered slowly, trying to find the right words. "They don't have the bag of gold."

"Then who does?" she gasped.

"I hid it," I admitted. "But now I can't get to it and I can't tell you where because it's too painful. If I write the secret down on that bit of paper, will you promise not to read it until you're out of town?"

She nodded, so I wrote:

*IT'S IN THE COFFIN. IT WAS THE ONLY PLACE
I COULD HIDE IT. I AM SORRY,
MARY JANE.*

It made my eyes water a little to write those words and when I folded the paper and passed it to Mary Jane, I saw that she was crying too. She shook my hand. "If I don't ever see you again," she sobbed, "I'll think of you often, and always say a prayer for you."

She was the bravest and most beautiful girl I had ever come across, and I never saw her again.

DOUBLE TROUBLE

They held the auction in the public square. It went on for most of the afternoon and everyone was still milling around watching the bidding when a big steamboat sounded its whistle out on the river. Five minutes later, I saw a crowd of people approaching, whooping and yelling and crying out: "Have you heard the news, boys? There are two more Wilks brothers in town. We've got two pairs now. You pays your money and you takes your choices which pair to believe."

At the front of the crowd, I could see an old gentleman with a kind expression on his face leading a younger man who had one arm in a sling. The townspeople were shouting and joking as though they'd been sipping whiskey all morning, but I didn't see anything funny about the situation. I was sure the duke and the king would turn white with fear when they noticed the procession, but they hardly batted an eyelid. The duke kept making his baby noises and smiling while the king pursed his lips and declared it was a shame that the world was full of such rascals and impostors. Most of the important local people quickly gathered around the king, to let him see they were on his side.

"This is an embarrassment for me, gentlemen," the old man at the front of the crowd began saying. I could tell at once he was speaking English the way they speak it in England, and nothing like the king's made-up accent. "We are the Wilks brothers, of course," he continued. "But we have been unlucky on our journey. My brother has broken his arm and our baggage has been sent to the wrong town. When our bags arrive, I can prove we are who we say we are. But, until that time, we shall go to the hotel and wait."

As he started off to the hotel with his brother, the king laughed out loud. "Broken his arm?" he boomed, so that everyone in the crowd could hear him. "I suppose that means he can't make any hand signals, doesn't it? That's convenient for a fraudster – almost as convenient as losing the baggage."

He started laughing again and most of the townspeople joined in. But I could see the doctor at the edge of the throng, talking to a thin man I didn't recognize. They were both nodding their heads and pointing at the king. A big, rough-looking fellow soon joined them. "Hey," the big man suddenly called to the king. "When did you get into town?"

"The day before the funeral, friend," the king replied calmly. "I came on a steamboat from Cincinnati."

"Then what were you doing upriver in the morning? In a canoe?"

"I was never in a canoe."

"That's a lie," cried the man to the crowd. "I live up there and I saw him with a boy in a canoe."

"Would you know that boy again?" the doctor asked him.

"He's standing right there," answered the man, pointing straight at me.

The crowd bayed like a pack of hounds when they heard this and the doctor held up his arms and said he was going to hold a trial. "Let's take all these Wilks brothers up to the hotel," he shouted, "and find out the truth."

The hotel manager cleared his lobby and set up some tables. It was after sunset so he brought out candles to light the proceedings. The duke, the king and I sat in a row of chairs on one side of the room, facing the new brothers on the other. Dr. Robinson prowled between us like a tiger pacing around his cage.

"Let's start with the gold," he snapped. "I think it would be wise to bring the money here, in case an accomplice of the fraudsters makes off with it. If this gentleman is honest," he cried, staring at the king, "he can't object to me sending for the money."

"Indeed not," replied the king. "But I regret, the money has been stolen. The slaves we sold took it. My servant can tell you everything."

The whole roomful of people started muttering and whispering, but the doctor waved a hand for silence.

"Did you see the slaves take the money?" he asked me softly.

"No, sir," I answered. "I saw them sneaking out of the room, nothing else."

"Boy, are you *really* an Englishman?"

When I said 'yes' he laughed in my face. The thin man he'd been talking to earlier stood up and walked over.

"Don't bother telling any more lies, boy," the thin man said to me. "I don't think you've had enough practice at it and you should take that as a compliment. I'm Levi Bell," he explained, "and I was Peter Wilks' lawyer. I was in St. Louis on business, but the doctor called me back to town and I'm sure glad he did. I landed on the steamboat with the new Wilks brothers. Well, we've wasted enough time asking all these questions. I want to get to the bottom of this fraud and I know just how to do it."

He picked up a pen and paper from one of the tables. "Peter Wilks was a man who liked to pen a letter," he drawled, "and so was Harvey. I have one of his notes from England in my carpetbag. Gentlemen, please sign your names on this paper. We can compare your signatures and reveal the cheats."

The duke gulped like a man dying of thirst, but the king was as bold as ever. He was reaching slowly for a pen, ready to bluff his way through the test, when the real Harvey Wilks suddenly jumped out of his chair.

"Gentlemen," he cried. "I can't allow it. My own writing is so hard to read, I always ask William to write my letters. And, as you know, his arm is broken."

Well, the king snorted in triumph and the duke gave me a grin and nudged my knee. He must have thought we were out of the woods. But the real Harvey hadn't finished talking. "I have another idea," he said meekly and turned to the king. "Can you tell me, sir," he asked, "what was the tattoo on my brother's chest?"

The king would have fallen over with shock if he hadn't been sitting down. All the blood ran out of his face and I was sure he'd confess everything that second, but he was tougher than he looked. "There is a small, blue arrow on his breast," he replied.

"It's a lie," the real Harvey shouted. "The letter 'P' is marked on his skin and nothing else."

Suddenly everyone in the lobby was shouting and roaring. "They're all crooks," called out one man. "Let's tar and feather all four."

"No," cried the lawyer. "I know the answer to this riddle. Let's get out to the graveyard and dig up the body. And if we don't find any marks on poor old Peter, we can lynch the lot of them."

The crowd swarmed around us and the big fellow who had spoken out against the king took me by the wrist and led me outside. He was as strong as Goliath and I had to run to keep up with him as he dragged me along. The doctor and the lawyer took up their positions at the front and we charged out of town to the graveyard, a mile downriver. Just about everyone who lived in the town came out to join the march – except for Mary Jane. I wished I hadn't told her to stay away until eleven o'clock, because she could have cleared my name in a second.

We hurried along the river road with some of the men screaming like wild cats. As if I wasn't scared enough by the trial and all the talk of lynching, the night sky began to cloud over and turn purple as a storm blew in. I saw the lightning winking and flashing over the hills and soon the wind was making the leaves tremble in the woods.

I had never been in this kind of trouble before, mixed up with real desperados and an angry mob. All my careful planning had come to nothing. Instead of escaping downriver with Jim, my life was hanging by a thread – at the mercy of some tattoo marks on a dead person.

I couldn't bear to think about it, but I couldn't think of anything else. Of course, I knew the king had been bluffing about the blue arrow tattoo. He was just stalling and waiting for a chance to run. It was getting darker and darker as the storm approached. This was the ideal moment to slip away from the crowd, but that Goliath's grip was like a band of steel and I was trapped.

The mob reached the cemetery and streamed around the headstones towards the new grave. They had brought dozens of shovels, but nobody had thought to carry a lantern. The doctor sent a man to the nearest house to get one, while a group of men started digging in the darkness

with the flicker of lightning guiding their shovels.

They dug and dug and the rain started to come down as the storm set in. When the lightning flashed you could see every man's face in that big crowd and the shovelfuls of dirt sailing up out of the grave. But the next second it was too dark to see anything at all.

At last they got the coffin out and began to unscrew the lid. Goliath pulled me forward, trying to get a better view in the gloom. All of a sudden the lightning cracked closer than ever and a man shrieked: "Boys, there's a bag of gold in here."

Goliath let out an excited whoop and ran forward, dropping my wrist so he could push his way through to the coffin. I was out on the river road before anyone knew I was gone, running like a hare.

I had that road all to myself and I flew along it. When I got to the town I ran straight up the main street to the Wilks' house. There was no light in Mary Jane's window and I was sorry – I don't know why. But, just as I was running by, I saw a candle glimmering and my heart swelled up as though it would burst. The next second the house was behind me and I ran on, plunging into the dark.

I stole a canoe and started paddling out to the island where Jim had been hiding all this time with our raft. "Out with you, Jim," I cried as I sprung aboard. "Set her loose. We're free of those crooks, Jim, let's get going."

Naturally, Jim wanted to know everything that had happened, but I said it could wait until we were a few miles downriver. There was nothing better than to be back with Jim and free of those rascals. I was so happy, I was skipping around the raft. But then the lightning flashed and I saw something that made my blood run cold. The duke and the king were on the river in a skiff, rowing in our direction with all their strength. I almost burst out crying.

As they climbed aboard, the king grabbed me by the collar. "Trying to give us the slip, were you?" he snarled.

"No, Your Majesty," I pleaded. "I had a chance to run and I took it. There was nothing I could do to save you, and what was the point of me staying there to be hung? When I got back here, I told Jim to hurry because I didn't want to be caught. We thought you were already dead and we were overcome with joy when we saw you coming."

"I should drown you for your lies," hissed the king.

"Oh, let him go," cried the duke. "I don't remember you asking after the boy when you got your chance to run."

"I curse that town and everyone in it," snapped the king, releasing me.

"Curse yourself while you're at it," the duke told him. "The only smart idea you've had lately was the tall story about a blue arrow on Wilks' chest. That bold lie bought us some time and saved us from the penitentiary."

They were both quiet for a minute, thinking over the events of the night.

"And to think we thought the slaves stole the gold," mumbled the king. "There's a mystery, don't you reckon, Bilgewater?"

"Do you take me for a fool?" the duke replied sternly. "I know who put that money in the coffin."

I moved a step closer to the edge of the raft.

"It was you, Your Majesty," the duke said with a scowl. He ran forward and grabbed the king by his neck. "Admit it, you old schemer," he shouted. "You thought you'd come back on your own one day and dig it up."

The king twisted and kicked. He accused the duke of hiding the money himself and he swore on his life that he was innocent. But, all the time, the duke's hands were choking him. He finally coughed out a confession.

"I did it," wheezed the king. "Now let me go, I beg you."

"Don't ever deny it again," snapped the duke. "I can live with a crook, but not with a liar. You even persuaded me to put all the money from my theatrical con into the pot, you crafty rat."

"But duke," the king whined. "It was you who suggested we do that."

"Not another word," yelled the duke, raising a fist in the air. "If you'd listened to me, we'd be rich. Instead, those girls have got more money than they started with – our money. Now get out of my sight."

The king skulked off to the wigwam and I heard him sucking on his whiskey bottle. Not long after, the duke joined him and soon they were both so drunk they decided to bury the hatchet and be partners again. When they were fast asleep and snoring, I told Jim the whole story.

HARD CHOICES

We made swift progress downriver, not daring to stop at a town for several days. The raft had come a long way south by now and we were in warm weather country. I noticed trees with clumps of feathery Spanish moss hanging from their branches and it made the woods look creepy and solemn. This was the first time I'd ever seen the moss, and the sight of it reminded me how far I was from home.

When the swindlers decided we were 'in the clear' they began trying their schemes again. But they hit a run of bad luck and none of their frauds made them any loot. Flat broke and feeling blue, they stopped going ashore and just lazed around the raft, plotting and whispering.

Jim and I didn't like the look of it. We thought they must be planning a murder or a robbery and we decided to give them the slip the first chance we got.

Early one morning, we hid the raft in a safe place about two miles below a shabby village called Pikesville. The king said he wanted to nose around the town and see if the inhabitants had been warned about the theatrical con. If they hadn't, he said he'd hire a stage. "If I'm not back by midday," he chuckled, "then we'll be putting on a show tonight. You'll know it's safe to come into town."

The duke was grumpy and sour all morning, fidgeting around the raft. He scolded us for everything we did until we couldn't move a finger without him barking orders at us. Although I was nervous about leaving Jim and the raft, it was a relief when the king didn't arrive and we could walk into town. I thought a change of scene might ease the duke's temper, and secretly I was hoping a chance might come up for Jim and me to escape.

It took us almost an hour to find the old king, hunched over in the back room of a squalid little tavern. He was as drunk as a lord and had a group of loafers teasing and baiting him. The king cursed and threatened them in a proud voice, but he was so tight he couldn't even stand up.

"You look a sorry mess, Your Majesty," cried the duke. "I thought you were taking care of business."

The king glared back, calling the duke a string of dirty names. That was the last straw for Bilgewater. He jumped on the king and started beating him around the head. I shot out of that saloon and ran down to the river road, fast as a deer. This was our chance to get away and I never wanted to set eyes on the king and duke as long as I lived.

"Set her loose, Jim, we're leaving," I called, when I got down to the water. But there was no answer. I checked the wigwam and then I darted into the woods, calling his name and whistling. But it was no use – Jim was gone.

I sat down and cried for a full minute and then I pulled myself together. Weeping in the woods wasn't going to get Jim back, so I ran out to the road, trying to think of a plan. I spotted a young boy walking away from me down the road and I caught up with him.

"Have you seen a slave lurking around here?" I asked him, and described Jim and the clothes he was wearing.

"He's down at Silas Phelps' place," the boy replied calmly. "He's a runaway. Are you with him?"

"Not if I can help it," I lied. "I came across him in the woods an hour ago and he said he'd skin me alive if I made a sound. He told me to stay where I was until he was out of sight. I was too afraid to move until I saw you passing by."

"Well," the boy smiled, "you don't have to be scared now. They've caught him. He's a runaway from New Orleans."

"It's a good job they got him," I gasped.

"It sure is," said the boy, adding in a confidential whisper: "He's worth two hundred dollars in reward money. I wish I'd met him out on the road with my pap. Or armed with a shotgun."

"Me too," I said. "But he was too big for a boy to tackle on his own. Who brought him in?"

"It was an old man, a stranger," whispered the boy. "He sold out his claim in the slave for forty dollars. I think he was too busy to go downriver to collect the reward money himself."

"That's funny," I cried, trying not to show how angry I was with that rat, the king. "Why would he miss out on all that extra money? Do you think that slave might not be a runaway?"

"Oh, but he is," the boy laughed. "I've seen his wanted poster and it describes him in every particular. He's going back to slaving in the plantations, and that's a fact."

I left the country boy and returned to the wigwam. My head was spinning so much I could hardly think straight. After all the weeks together on the raft, and after everything we'd done for them, those scoundrels had ruined everything for Jim and me. They had made my friend a slave again – for the rest of his life – and all for forty, dirty dollars.

I tried to think of a plan but I couldn't see any way out of our troubles. If I wrote to Miss Watson she might claim Jim back and then at least he would be home with his friends. But why would she want to keep him, when she had been happy to sell him in the first place? Jim would still wind up in New Orleans.

Then I started thinking about all my friends in St. Petersburg and what they would say when they heard Huck Finn had helped a slave to escape. My conscience began pestering me, scolding me for my silence on the river when I had met the two slave hunters. The guilt welled up in me like a river rise. Was Jim's arrest a message for me from the good place I wondered? I was so scared I started shaking. Perhaps I deserved to be punished, for helping Jim and robbing poor Miss

Watson out of her eight hundred dollars? All of a sudden I felt sick with guilt, so I kneeled down on the raft and tried to pray.

I knew what I had to say. I had to promise that I would write to Miss Watson and return Jim to slavery where he belonged. But I couldn't get the words out of my mouth. Deep down in my heart I didn't want to see Jim in chains again. I couldn't pray for something that was a lie.

I had never been so confused in all my life. My conscience told me to confess and send Jim back, but my heart wouldn't let me. Thinking that it might help me to do the right thing, I decided to write the letter. Then I could have another try at praying. I found a scrap of paper and wrote:

Miss Watson, your slave Jim is two miles below Pikesville with a Mr. Phelps. Send your reward.
HUCK FINN

For the first time in my life I felt washed clean of my sins and I was ready to pray. But, before I tried, I put the paper down and started to think. At first, I was thinking how lucky I was, to have written the note and saved myself from going to hell. But then I thought of my friend Jim and our long journey down the river. I saw him standing before me, riding through storms and high water. I remembered how he always took the night watch, and sometimes did my watch as well, just so I could go on sleeping. He was always laughing, and smiling and trying to put my mind at rest. Then I thought of the time in the fog, when he spent all night worrying and fretting that I might be hurt. I couldn't think of a single occasion when he was mean or vicious to me, and I could hear his words when we thought we were coming down to Cairo: "Huck, you're my best friend. You're my *only* friend in the world." Then I looked down at that grubby little piece of paper addressed to Miss Watson.

I picked it up, with my fingers trembling, because I had to make a decision that would either damn me or save me. I held my breath, then I said to myself: "All right then, I'll go to hell."

And I tore it up.

There can't be a harder choice than that, but I never tried to take those words back. Huck Finn wasn't the reforming type, I decided, and what my heart wanted was to set Jim free.

I turned over a few plans in my head and at last I came up with one I liked. When it got dark, I took the raft over to an island and hid it in some trees. I had a good sleep and when the sun came up I got dressed in my best clothes and paddled the canoe downriver. After two miles I landed and hid the canoe in some bushes, in case I needed her again.

There was a track running along the bank and I followed it until I saw a sign: *Phelps' Sawmill*. I spotted the farmhouse set back from the road, but I wasn't ready to go there yet so I pushed on into town.

Turning a corner, I walked straight into the duke, sticking up a poster for his acting con.

"Where did you spring from?" he gasped, looking astonished to see me. "And where's the raft?"

"That's just what I was going to ask you," I replied, thinking quickly. "After I left you in the tavern, I thought I'd look around town," I lied. "But a man offered me ten cents to herd some sheep and it took me most of the day to do it. When I went back to the raft, she was gone, and so was my slave. He was the only property I had in the world, duke. It broke my heart to lose him. I fell asleep in the woods and I've just come into town to look for him."

"Well, don't ask me," cried the duke in a sudden rage. "Where's our raft, boy? That old fool sold your slave for forty dollars and gambled it all away with those loafers in the saloon. It took me most of the day to sober him up, and when we found the raft was gone we thought you'd cut out on us."

"Why would I run away without *my* slave?" I said craftily.

"I suppose that makes sense," he answered, scratching his chin. "But we passed so much time with that slave, we started thinking he was ours. Now we haven't got a dime and there's nothing to do but try the show again. Have you got any money, boy? I've been longing for a drink all day."

I gave him ten cents and begged him to spend it on food for us to share. "It's all I own in the world," I whimpered (even though I had all those dollars stitched away in my clothes). "I'm hungry and I've got nothing left. Where's my slave?"

"He's not your slave any more," laughed the duke. "But if you swear to keep your mouth shut for the next three days, I'll tell you where he is. You might be able to bargain him back somehow."

"I won't say a word about you or the king, duke," I promised.

"It was a man called Foster who bought him," the duke lied. "He lives forty miles away, back in the woods. Just take the main road through town and you can't miss his farm."

I knew that rascal was trying to get me out of the way for three or four days so he could make his escape with the ticket money, but I played along with him. "I'll start walking right away," I said.

"You do that," he chuckled. "And don't break your promise. If you say a word about us, I'll track you down if it takes me a whole year to find you."

He watched me for a mile or more as I tramped along the main road. When the track ran out of sight behind a low hill, I slipped into the trees and doubled back to the Phelps' farmhouse.

THE ESCAPE ARTISTS

It was all still and Sunday-like when I reached the farm. The slaves had gone out to work in the fields and it was so quiet I could hear the flies buzzing and the leaves whispering in the woods.

The Phelps farm was one of those lonely, one-horse cotton plantations that all look alike. There was a wood-post fence snaking around two acres of dirt yard, and standing in the middle was a big log house for all the family. At the back of the house I could see a smokehouse, a small hut and some cabins for the slaves. All these buildings had been whitewashed once, but it must have been back in the days of Noah. I could see a little bench by the kitchen door, and a bucket of water with a cup lying next to it. A hound lay out in the sun, fast asleep. Beyond the dog there was a watermelon patch and a vegetable garden and then the cotton fields began. The woods sprouted up where the fields ended, thick and dark to the horizon.

I hopped over the fence and started strolling over to the kitchen. When I was halfway across the yard I noticed the hum of a spinning wheel – a lonely, whirring noise in all the silence of the woods. Then I heard a growl and when I turned around I saw a big dog following my tracks. Dogs came running from every corner of the yard. I knew the safest thing to do was to stand stock-still and meet their stares. In just a few seconds, snarling hounds surrounded me. It was as if I was the hub of a wheel and the spokes were made up of barking dogs.

One of the house slaves came dashing out from the kitchen and saved me. She had a rolling pin in one hand and she gave the biggest dog a great clout on the side of his head, shouting: "Get off him, Tiger, get going." When the hounds settled down they came over to me and started licking my hands and wagging their tails. Dogs are always friendly if you treat them the right way.

I looked up and saw more slaves running out to see what all the noise was about. They were soon joined by a woman in her forties, who I guessed was the farmer's wife. She was waving a spinning-stick in one hand and reaching out to me with the other.

"It's you, at last," she cried, with a big smile on her face.

I nodded my head without thinking.

"I knew it," she yelled, hugging me tightly. The tears were running down her cheeks and I was too amazed to say anything. "You don't look much like your mother," she told me. "But I'm so glad to see you, Tom. Oh, children," she called to some youngsters hiding in the kitchen, "don't dawdle there. Come out and meet your cousin, Tom."

But they were too scared to leave the safety of the house.

"You must be hungry," she said, turning back to face me. "Did you have any breakfast on the boat?"

I nodded my head once more.

"Come into the house," she ordered, tugging on my hand. "It's been years since I've seen you, and here you are at last. We've been expecting you on the steamboat for two days or more. What kept you? Did the boat run aground and get delayed?"

"Yes ma'am," I gulped, sitting down on an old wooden chair in the kitchen.

"Don't call me that, it's too formal," she laughed. "Call me Aunt Sally. Where did it happen?"

I had no idea if Tom's boat was coming up the river or down. My instinct told me it must have departed from New Orleans but I didn't know any of the place names along that stretch of the river. Then I had an idea. "It wasn't the grounding that slowed us, Aunt Sally. Something in the engine room blew up."

"Goodness," she cried. "Your uncle Silas was on a boat last year and two men died in an engine explosion. Your uncle's been up to town every day to meet you. He left again only an hour ago. Did you meet him on the road?"

"My boat landed at dawn," I told her. "I left all my luggage at the wharf and went for a walk in the woods to pass the time. I thought it would be rude to wake you up too early, so I didn't come along the river road."

"Who's got your baggage?" she asked.

"I hid it, Aunt."

"And how did you get any breakfast before first light?"

"The captain saw me hanging around on deck and he offered me some grub in the officers' cabin."

I kept glancing over at the children, trying to think of some excuse to steal away and talk with them in private – to discover who I was supposed to be. But I couldn't escape from Mrs. Phelps' interrogation. When she started asking me questions about my family, I could feel beads of cold sweat streaking down my back.

"Tell me everything," she demanded, waving the spinning-stick in my face. "I've been so selfish, carrying on about all my concerns. Give me the family gossip and don't scrimp or miss out a thing."

I didn't see how I could fool her with any more of my lies. But, just as I was preparing to tell her the

whole truth, she grabbed my shoulders and pushed me to the floor.

"Quick, boy, hide under the table," she whispered. "I can see Silas out in the yard and I want to play a joke on him. Don't make a sound."

I had a glimpse of the old gentleman as he stepped into the room, then Mrs. Phelps wrapped her arms around him. "Has he come?" she wailed.

"No," said Mr. Phelps, flatly.

"But where can he be?" she howled.

"I don't know and it's making me uneasy," replied Silas. "I'm at my wit's end. Something bad must have happened to the boat."

"Why, Silas?" she cried, pointing out through the open door. "Is that someone coming along the road?"

He whirled around to look and Mrs. Phelps yanked me out from under the table. When he turned back, I was standing before him and his face was beaming and smiling like a house on fire.

"Who's this?" he gasped.

"Why, darling," she cried, "it's Tom Sawyer, of course."

My legs started wobbling and I would have hit the floor if Mr. Phelps hadn't grabbed my hand. He shook it until I thought my arm would come off. Then everyone was laughing and smiling and relieved – most of all, me. I was so glad to find out who I was. It didn't matter if they quizzed me for three days straight, I knew enough about the Sawyer family to talk until my chin stopped working.

There was only one thing that made me nervous. Suddenly I heard a steamboat whistle out on the river and realized that the real Tom Sawyer could walk in on us any second. I knew Tom would be as eager as mustard to help me with a scheme, but I had to catch him *before* he spoke with the Phelps.

So, I asked my new aunt and uncle if I could borrow their horse and cart to go into town to get my luggage. Silas wanted to take me himself but I insisted: "I've troubled you enough, uncle." Before he could argue, I had rushed outside to harness his horse.

When I was halfway to town I saw another wagon approaching. I reined my horse and waited for it to come up and, sure enough, Tom Sawyer stopped alongside me. His mouth opened like the lid of a trunk and he swallowed so loud I could hear it.

"I never did you any harm," he whispered, with a guilty look. "You know that's true. So why do you want to come back and haunt me?"

"I was never gone, Tom," I chuckled.

When he heard my voice he cheered up a bit, but he wasn't quite satisfied. "Don't trick me," he said. "Tell me true, are you a ghost?"

"No more than you are," I told him.

"But weren't you murdered?" he asked.

"Not that I know of. I played a trick on pap at the cabin. Come over and pinch my arm if you don't believe me."

He did just that, and when he was convinced I was alive and well, he started firing questions at me. But it wasn't the time or the place to tell him about my adventures, so I asked his driver to wait and I led Tom into the woods. When we were away from the road I explained my fix at the Phelps' house.

"Don't say anything for two minutes," he commanded. "This is a real quandary, Huck, and I have to think it through."

Two minutes later he jumped up and announced he had a plan.

"Take my trunk back to the house," he said quickly, "and pretend it's yours. I'm going to wait out here for a while and arrive after you. Don't behave as though you know who I am when I walk in."

"Tom," I interrupted. "There's something else you have to know. There's a slave at the Phelps' house, Miss Watson's Jim, do you remember him? I'm trying to steal him out of slavery."

131

"What?" he gasped. "But don't you know Jim is..."

He stopped and stared down at the ground, thinking things over.

"I know it shocks you, Tom," I said. "But I'm going to steal him and I want you to keep it a secret."

His eyes lit up and he declared: "No, Huck. I'll help you steal him."

I was astonished to hear him say that, and I have to say Tom Sawyer fell right down in my estimation. I couldn't believe he would join me in such wickedness. "You're joking, Tom?" I said.

"No joke," he answered. "So put my trunk in your wagon and I'll see you up at the house, shortly."

Tom arrived thirty minutes after I pulled into the yard. Aunt Sally spotted him from the kitchen window.

"There's a stranger out there, Silas," she called to her husband. "We'd better put another plate on for dinner."

Everybody rushed to the kitchen door to get a peek at the mystery guest and I saw Tom vault over a stile in the fence and wave a "goodbye" to his wagon driver. I had to smile as I watched him walk proudly up to the door and lift his hat with all the pomp and ceremony of Robin Hood meeting his Maid Marian.

"No, my boy," Silas replied. "Archie Nichols lives another three miles down the road. But please come in. You can have dinner with us and I'll take you over to Archie's later."

"I can't ask you to do that," Tom protested. "I can walk."

"Haven't you ever heard of southern hospitality?" said Silas, with a wink. Step inside."

Tom took a stride into the room and announced he was William Thompson from Hicksville, Ohio. He made a bow. Then he reached over and planted a big kiss on Aunt Sally's lips and sat down on a chair.

"Why, you mischievous puppy," she shrieked. "What do you mean by kissing me?"

"I thought you'd want me to, madam," Tom replied innocently.

"Why, were you born a fool?" she asked him, picking up the first weapon she could find – her spinning-stick – and wiggling it barely an inch from his nose. "What made you think I'd want you to do that?"

"They told me you would," said Tom.

"Well, *they* must be lunatics like you," she cried. "Tell me their names."

Tom got to his feet and fumbled with his hat, looking pained. "I swear I won't do it again, ma'am," he said. "At least, not until you ask me to."

"Ask you to?" she screeched. "Why would I want that?"

"Because I'm Sid Sawyer," said Tom and he hooted with laughter.

"Tom's brother, why you little rascal," she cried with happiness, reaching out to hug him.

"You have to ask me for a kiss first," joked Tom. And she did.

"We weren't expecting both Sawyer brothers to visit," Aunt Sally explained when all the hugging and kissing was finally over. "But it's a joy to see you, Sid."

"I begged and begged," Tom explained. "At the last minute, mother said I could come too and we cooked up this prank to give you a double surprise. But I never thought it would be so dangerous in Aunt Sally's house." He picked up the spinning-stick and smiled.

"You gave me a shock, I have to admit it," Aunt Sally laughed. "But I thought it was Tom who was the practical joker and adventurer? Sid always sounded like a serious child."

"I like a good joke too," replied Tom, nudging my foot under the table. "Now, did somebody mention dinner?"

It was so comfortable being back in a friendly, peaceful household, I almost forgot about my dangerous adventures on the river. Then, at supper that evening, one of the children said something that made me prick up my ears.

"Can I take Tom and Sid to the show tonight, pap?" asked the eldest boy.

"There won't be any show," Silas replied. "The runaway slave told me all about that scandalous performance and I've warned the sheriff. I reckon the townspeople will have taken care of those two loafers by now."

Even after everything those two grifters had done to Jim and me, I still didn't want to see them torn apart by a mob. Somebody needed to warn them. Tom and I were sharing a room in the farmhouse and as soon as we got upstairs I told him all about the king and the duke. We shinned down the lightning rod on the wall outside our window and dashed into town.

As we got closer we saw a crowd of people rushing along the road in a rage. Some of them carried torches; others were banging tin pans and blowing horns. We jumped to one side to let them pass and I saw two large shapes bobbing along in the middle of the crowd, tied to a rail. It was the king and the duke, I realized, although they didn't look anything like men. The mob had coated them in tar and rolled them in feathers. It made me sick to see it and I was sorry for those rascals. Human beings can be so cruel to one another.

My conscience kept gnawing at me as we walked back home. I wasn't responsible for the sufferings of the duke and the king, but I felt somehow to blame. It's always that way with your conscience, I decided. Whether you do right or wrong, it has a way of making you feel like a skunk.

We were stumbling along in the dark when Tom Sawyer suddenly blurted out: "I've got it, Huck. I know where Jim is."

"Where?" I cried.

"Did you notice a slave take a bowl of food over to the hut in the yard this afternoon?" he asked me.

"Uh-huh," I replied. "He was feeding a dog."

"No, he wasn't," Tom continued. "There was some watermelon in that bowl and dogs don't eat watermelon. And there's a padlock on that hut. It's got to be the prison."

That's what made Tom Sawyer special. He had a way of seeing things that made other people look short-sighted.

"I think I've got my escape plan almost ready," he said boldly.

"But Tom," I replied, "are you sure you want to help me? You've got a good reputation and family back in St. Petersburg. I don't want to drag you down with me."

"I know what I'm doing," Tom barked. "Don't I always know what I'm doing, Huck?"

"You sure do, Tom," I agreed. I didn't try to warn him off again.

It was close to midnight by the time we got back and the Phelps' house was dark and still. We went straight down to investigate the hut. None of the dogs bothered us because they knew we were friendly. We saw that the door was padlocked and the only other way in was through a small high window that had been boarded up. At the back of the hut there was a lean-to shed that was padlocked too. Tom found an old piece of iron out in the yard and he used it to lever the ring that held the padlock out of the wood. The chain fell off and we slipped inside. There was nothing in there but rusty old tools and a dirt floor and, when our match went out, so did we. Tom fixed the staple and chain back in position and rubbed his hands with glee.

"We should have a first-rate adventure breaking Jim out," he whispered.

In the morning we wandered across to the slave cabins and tried to strike up a conversation with the man who carried the food to the hut.

"Must be a large dog in that hut," drawled Tom, when we'd been chatting with the man for a minute or two. "He always gets a big plateful of food."

"He's a large one," said the man, grinning. "Do you want to see him?"

"Why not?" replied Tom casually, and he ignored the nervous glances I was shooting at him.

He led us down to the hut and yanked the door open. It was too dark for my eyes to see anything at first, but when I stepped inside I saw Jim sitting on an old spring bed.

"Why Huck!" he cried out when he saw me. "And is that you, Tom Sawyer?"

"Wait one second," yelled the Phelps' slave. "Do you gentlemen all know each other?"

Tom turned and looked at him as though he was a doctor examining a patient. "Are you feverish?" Tom asked. "We didn't say anything, did we Sid?"

I shook my head.

"Have we met before?" Tom asked Jim, and Jim was wise enough to deny it.

"I must be mistaken," the man grumbled.

"Here's a dime," said Tom, passing him a coin. "Buy some ointment for your ears."

The slave went out into the light, to have a look at the dime. I just had time to squeeze Jim's hand and say, "We're getting you out," before he came back and called us away.

Tom guided me out to the woods that afternoon to discuss his plan.

"There's a problem," he began by saying.

"What's that?" I asked, puzzled that the great Tom Sawyer had hit a snag.

"It's too easy," he said. "There should be a moat around the hut, or a watchman, or a pack of wolves guarding the door."

"What are you getting at, Tom?" I gasped.

"There's not enough of a challenge for me," he complained. "For a great escape plan, you need to overcome impossible obstacles and incredible risks. I want to send the prisoner files in pies, and rope ladders, and have drawbridges and metal spikes slamming down at the last second so they almost clip our ankles."

"What are you talking about, Tom?"

"It's all in the books, Huck," he sighed. "Men chew their own legs off to get out of their dungeon cells."

"We're not chewing Jim's leg off," I snapped. "Let's just dig him out with the tools in the shed."

"We can't do that, Huck," he replied angrily. "Any fool could dig him out with a spade. We'll use our bare hands."

"But that might take weeks."

"In the books they work at their escape plans for thirty years or more. And they keep a tally of the days on the wall of their cell, with a rusty nail. In their own blood sometimes."

"Can't we just use our knives?" I pleaded. "That will still be a challenge and we won't break our fingers digging."

Tom said that might be acceptable.

It took two nights of digging with picks and shovels to finish the hole under Jim's hut. We did try with the knives, but our fingers were soon torn and blistered. Tom said we could use the other tools, but we had to *pretend* they were knives. That was almost as good, he told me later.

Jim cried over us when we crawled into his prison. He said he wanted to escape right away, but Tom begged him to be patient. "We'll get you away, don't you worry," he purred. "But we have to do it properly."

I don't think Jim or I understood why we couldn't just make a dash for it. But we knew Tom Sawyer always had his own way of going about things, and we trusted him.

"Say, Jim," said Tom, "Have you got any spiders in here?"

"No, I haven't," laughed Jim. "And I hate spiders almost as much as I hate snakes."

Tom was mumbling and pondering for a minute or two and then he said: "That's a good idea. It's just what we need. Every dungeon has to have some snakes."

The next day we were out in the woods collecting

snakes. Tom wanted us to use rattlers, but Jim said it was painful enough to share his prison cell with any reptile, let alone one that might kill him. We snared two dozen garter snakes, that had no venom, and we put them in a sack under our bed and went down for dinner. But Tom didn't tie the sack properly and the snakes wriggled free. For a few days we had snakes popping up all over the house, dripping from the rafters and landing in your dinner plate. Aunt Sally had the worst time of it because she loathed snakes. If one dropped onto her head, as they did from time to time, she just screamed and ran out into the yard.

Jim didn't like the other snakes we caught for his hut either, but he put up with it. He was a patient man, Jim.

"We're ready to go tomorrow," Tom finally announced, when we were sitting with Jim in the hut one evening. "All we need now is the dress and the warning letter."

"A dress?" I gulped.

"It's Jim's disguise," Tom explained. "Escaping prisoners always wear ladies clothes when they slip out of the castle."

"We can take one of Aunt Sally's," I suggested. "What's this letter we need?"

Tom showed us a note he had prepared. It read:

Beware. Keep a sharp lookout at midnight.
A FRIEND

"But Tom," I cried. "Doesn't that make our job all the harder?"

"Naturally," he smiled. "I'll be out most of the day, seeing to the final arrangements for my plan. I'll meet you in the hut at midnight."

The Phelps family were terrified when they got that note. The next day they asked all the local farmers to come around with their guns. In the evening I saw at least fifteen armed men chatting and smoking in the sitting room. Aunt Sally kept asking me to help serve them food and drinks and it was only ten minutes before midnight when I finally managed to sneak outside. I thought Tom would be sure to call his escape plan off, when I told him about the armed guards in the house.

Inside the hut it was black as pitch. "Are you here, boys?" I whispered.

"You're early," Tom hissed. "What's the matter?"

"The house is crammed with armed men," I told him.

"Wonderful," said Tom. "Let's get on with it."

We ducked down to get to the hole and I suddenly heard one of the farmers outside, trying the handle to the main door of the hut. "We came too early," said the man. "Let's hide in here and wait for them."

Tom squeezed through the hole to enter the lean-to. He forced the padlock off the lean-to door and we all tiptoed into the yard. I had to smile when I realized Jim was wearing one of Aunt Sally's old nightgowns.

"Who's that?" came a shout. "Answer, or I'll shoot."
We ran like deer for the river and I heard bullets
whizzing over our heads.

LIGHTING OUT

Half a mile down the river road, we found the canoe and started paddling for the raft.

"You're a free man again," I cried to Jim, as we hauled ourselves onto the raft.

"That's right," he laughed. "And we pulled off that escape in grand style."

We were all whooping with joy, but Tom was the happiest of all. He had a bullet buried in his calf.

"Don't stop now," he roared, when he saw our faces drop. "We've got to get on with the plan. Leave me the canoe and you can take the raft."

"No, Tom," said Jim gravely. "You need a doctor and you're not strong enough to go out on the river alone. I can't let you risk bleeding to death, even if it means getting caught and being a slave again."

Jim went off to hide in the woods while I set out for town in the canoe. I found a doctor and told him a story about my friend being hurt in a hunting accident, but try as I might he wouldn't step into the canoe with me.

"Tell me where your raft is, son," he asked me kindly, "and I'll row myself over there."

I had no choice but to do it. Then I went to sleep in the soft grass. I woke up in the morning with Uncle Silas shaking me by the shoulder.

When we got home, Aunt Sally was so glad to see me she cried. I told her that Sid and I had climbed down from our window when we heard the shots in the night. I said we had chased around in the woods and somehow got separated. But, when Tom Sawyer arrived in the yard in the back of a wagon, she knew this was all a lie. He was asleep, leaning against the doctor. Jim was walking behind the cart in chains, with an escort of armed men.

They threw Jim into the hut and they cursed him for trying to escape. But the doctor came over and spoke up for him. He said that Jim had helped him to take the bullet out of Tom's leg and stayed up nursing him all night long on the raft. "Tom might have died without this slave," the doctor declared.

I racked my brains thinking of how I would explain everything to the Phelps family when Tom recovered. But I was wasting my time. Tom confessed to everything, and he was proud of what we'd done. I could hardly believe my ears as he told a shocked Aunt Sally the whole story – including the part with the snakes – but I was in for an even greater surprise.

"What happened to Jim?" Tom asked. "Is he free?"

"No," Aunt Sally replied, sternly. "He's chained up in the hut."

"Take those chains off him," Tom yelled. "Jim's a

free man. Old Miss Watson never forgave herself for selling him to the New Orleans slaver. When she died two months ago, she granted him freedom in her will."

"Then why didn't you say so before?" cried Aunt Sally.

"I wanted the challenge," Tom Sawyer told her. "We needed a real adventure."

And he was still trying to explain himself when someone stepped into the room behind us.

"So it's you, Huck Finn," cried Tom's Aunt Polly. "I've come eleven hundred miles to find out what's been going on down here. And all the way I had a feeling you might be mixed up in it."

Tom always said he was going to tell Jim he was a free man, as soon as they reached the raft. But I reckon the bullet in his leg was making him a little crazy, and he was too excited about the escape plan to think straight.

Jim was out of his chains in no time and Tom gave him a reward of forty dollars for being such a patient prisoner. Then Tom told us we could join a new gang he was starting up, over in the New Territory wilderness.

"I like the sound of it, Tom," I told him, "but I haven't got the money for a horse and a gun. Pap must have taken all my savings by now."

"But nobody's seen him since you left," cried Tom. "Your money's still with the judge."

"Don't worry, Huck," Jim said mysteriously. "He won't ever be taking your money."

"What does that mean, Jim?" I gasped. He wouldn't tell me, so I had to pester it out of him.

"Do you remember the house we explored," he said

at last, "floating along the river? That was your pap in the room, I'm sorry, Huck."

Tom got better and made a good luck charm out of that bullet. He wears it on a chain around his neck. And that's all I've got to put down in this book, and I'm glad to say it, because it's caused me a lot of trouble, this writing business. And now I reckon I should make a run for it and light out for the Territory ahead of the rest, because Aunt Sally wants to adopt me and make me a civilized boy. I've been there before and I didn't like it.

THE END – YOURS TRULY,
HUCK FINN

ABOUT MARK TWAIN

Mark Twain was more than just a writer. He was a fictional character, created by a budding novelist, humorist and wit named, Samuel Langhorne Clemens. His books earned him a worldwide reputation and in the early 1900s he was one of America's most famous celebrities.

Clemens was born in 1835, the same year that Halley's comet streaked across the sky. He grew up in Hannibal, a small town in Missouri that provided the model for Huck's St. Petersburg. Many of the characters and story ideas in Clemens' later books came from memories of these boyhood years on the Mississippi River.

When the American Civil War broke out in 1861, Clemens volunteered for his local militia. But he deserted after only a few weeks. Rather than rejoin the army, he headed west with his brother, Orion. Clemens spent almost two weeks crossing the country in a rickety stagecoach, before arriving at a mining camp in Nevada. After drifting around the camps, looking for adventure and digging for gold, he got a job at a small local newspaper. Although Clemens had already tried his hand at several trades in Missouri –

printing, writing and working as a river pilot among them – he had never settled into an occupation. But sitting at his newspaper desk, he discovered that he had a flair for writing short, comic pieces and news reports. It was in 1863 that he began signing his work with the pen name, Mark Twain. *Mark Twain* was an expression used by Mississippi river pilots when checking the depth of a river with a weighted line.

Working as a journalist, Twain developed a writing style that combined spoof, satire and puzzlement. He understood that it was vital to entertain his audience, and his stories and book reviews poked fun at anyone who took themselves too seriously. But he still managed to slip serious discussions and arguments into his reports. Newspaper editors liked his work and in 1867 he was offered the chance to travel the world as a 'roving' reporter. He collected the articles describing the voyage into his first book, *Innocents Abroad* (1869). It was an immediate bestseller.

Twain bought a large house in Hartford, Connecticut and began work on his second novel, *Roughing It* (1872). This rambling comedy, describing his stagecoach journey across the west and prospecting around Nevada, was another success. Twain followed it with the books that ensured his literary reputation: *The Adventures of Tom Sawyer* (1876), *The Prince and the Pauper* (1881) and *The Adventures of Huckleberry Finn* (1885).

As his fame increased, Mark Twain began booking concert halls to give recitals of his work. He grew rich, although he went on to squander much of his wealth on a series of disastrous business ventures. But he was always able to make money from public speaking. He toured the world and even received an honorary degree from Oxford University in 1907 – one of the proudest achievements of his career.

The last years of Mark Twain's life were disrupted by family tragedy, as two of his daughters died suddenly. Heartbroken, the writer died in 1910, a year after the death of his youngest daughter. By coincidence, his death coincided with another visit by Halley's comet in the night sky.

FRANKENSTEIN

FROM THE STORY BY

MARY SHELLEY

He made his way to the tank and peeped over the rim. There was only the smooth, undisturbed surface of the liquid . . . Confused thoughts and troubled emotions ran through his mind. He had failed, it was true, but maybe that was for the best. He sighed and relaxed slightly. Then, from the liquid, a huge hand shot out to grab him.

As lightning flashes across the night sky, Victor Frankenstein succeeds in the ultimate scientific experiment – the creation of life. But the being he creates, though intelligent and sensitive, is so huge and hideous that it is rejected by its creator, and by everyone else who meets it. Soon, the lonely, miserable monster turns on Victor and his family, with terrifying and tragic results.

ANOTHER USBORNE CLASSIC

FROM THE STORY BY

CHARLOTTE BRÖNTE

Suddenly, a terrible, savage scream ripped
the night apart. It echoed the length of
Thornfield Hall, then died away, leaving
me fixed to the spot.

The scream had come from above and,
sure enough, as I listened, I heard the
sounds of a struggle in an attic room
upstairs. Then a muffled man's voice
shouted: "Help! Help! Help!"

A poor orphan, Jane Eyre is bullied by her rich relations
and sent away to school. Determined to change her
luck, she becomes a governess and settles happily into
a new life at Thornfield Hall. But why is Mr. Rochester,
her employer, so mysterious, and whose menacing laugh
does Jane keep hearing at night?

ANOTHER USBORNE CLASSIC

WUTHERING HEIGHTS

FROM THE STORY BY
EMILY BRÖNTE

... just as I was drifting off to sleep I became aware of a loud, insistent noise. Somewhere outside, a branch was knocking against the window, scratching and thumping in time to the wailing of the wind.

Eventually I could bear it no longer. I climbed out of bed, determined to break off the branch and put an end to the noise... but instead my fingers closed on a small, ice-cold hand!

High on the windswept Yorkshire moors, an old farmhouse hides dark secrets. What is the strange history of Wuthering Heights? Why has Heathcliff, its mysterious owner, cut himself off from the world, and who is the unearthly girl wandering the moors at night? The answers bring to light a passionate tale of two generations torn apart by love and revenge.

ANOTHER USBORNE CLASSIC

DR JEKYLL & MR HYDE

FROM THE STORY BY
ROBERT LOUIS STEVENSON

Behind the locked door of Dr. Jekyll's
laboratory lies a mystery his lawyer is
determined to solve. Why does the doctor
spend so much time there? What is the
connection between the respectable
Dr. Jekyll and his visitor, the loathsome
Mr. Hyde? Why has Jekyll changed his
will to Hyde's advantage? And who
murdered Sir Danvers Carew?

This spine-chilling retelling brings Robert Louis
Stevenson's classic horror story to life, and is
guaranteed to thrill and terrify modern readers as
much as when The Strange Case of Dr. Jekyll and
Mr. Hyde was first published over a century ago.

Another Usborne Classic

Dracula

FROM THE STORY BY

BRAM STOKER

When the other passengers on the
stagecoach found out where Jonathan
was going, they stared at him in
astonishment. Then they started
whispering in Transylvanian and
Jonathan heard some words that he
knew: *pokol* and *vrolok*. The first word
meant hell, and the second . . .
Jonathan shivered. It meant vampire.

When Jonathan Harker arrives at creepy Castle
Dracula in Transylvania, he has no idea what to
expect, but all too soon his host's horrible nocturnal
habits have him fearing for his life. . . This is the story
of a battle against the forces of evil, as the eccentric
Professor Van Helsing and his brave young friends
take on the vilest vampire in the world.

Another Usborne Classic

Tales of King Arthur

RETOLD BY

FELICITY BROOKS

A gleaming expanse of water lay before
them, with a huge, purple mountain
rising up behind it.

Arthur scanned the lake's silvery
surface, and without knowing why, he
found his eyes coming to rest on a spot in
the middle. Without any warning, a hand
suddenly shot up from beneath the water,
holding a jewel-covered sword and
scabbard, which sparkled in the sunlight.

Full of magic, mystery and suspense, these fast-
moving tales recount some of the most exciting
adventures of King Arthur and the Knights of the
Round Table. From the sword in the stone to the last
battle, these stories bring to life the characters of
Camelot: Merlin the wizard, gallant Sir Lancelot,
beautiful Queen Guinevere and evil Morgan le Fay.

Another Usborne Classic

MOBY DICK

FROM THE STORY BY
HERMAN MELVILLE

But while they relaxed on the surface,
Moby Dick was thundering towards
them, charging up from a thousand feet
below. The speeding whale smashed into
the hull of one boat and carried it forty
feet into the air. It burst into a cloud of
wood chips and broken, bloody men.

Longing to go to sea, Ishmael signs up for a voyage
on the whaling ship Pequod. The ship's captain,
Ahab, soon reveals his true mission. He wants
revenge on the whale that maimed him.
The chase takes Ishmael to the other side of the
world and ends in a terrifying fight for survival.